All I Want For Christmas Is A Reaper

LIANA BROOKS

OTHER WORKS

ALL I WANT FOR CHRISTMAS

All I Want For Christmas Is A Reaper
All I Want For Christmas Is A Werewolf

FLEET OF MALIK

Bodies In Motion
Change of Momentum

HEROES AND VILLAINS

Even Villains Fall In Love
Even Villains Go To The Movies
Even Villains Have Interns
Even Villains Play The Hero (omnibus)
The Polar Terror

TIME AND SHADOWS

The Day Before
Convergence Point
Decoherence

SHORTER WORKS

Fey Lights
Prime Sensations
Darkness and Good

Find other works by the author at www.lianabrooks.com

All I Want For Christmas Is A

Reaper

LIANA BROOKS

AUSTRALIA

Print ISBN: 978-1-922434-03-6
eBook ISBN: 9781393919186

www.inkprintpress.com

National Library of Australia Cataloguing-in-Publication Data
Brooks, Liana 1982—
All I Want For Christmas Is A Reaper (Kickstarter Edition)
218 p.   cm.
ISBN: 978-1-922434-04-3
Inkprint Press, Canberra, Australia
1. Fiction—Romance—Paranormal—General 2. Fiction—Fantasy—Paranormal 3. Fiction—Romance—Workplace 4. Fiction—Holidays

Summary: Merri Kriesmas, Grim Reaper of Chicago, comes to Cozy Studies to audit their accounts and finds the love of her life.

First Edition: December 2020

Cover design © Inkprint Press.

This is for everyone who is happy they aren't where they used to be.

ALL I WANT FOR CHRISTMAS IS A REAPER

THREE O'CLOCK ON A THURSDAY AFTERNOON IN APRIL, and I had an unplanned three-day weekend. In Chicago, my favorite city in the world. There were thunderheads gathering over Lake Michigan with the smell of rain in the air but, for now, downtown was a delightful playground of rushing cars, stressed commuters, and the bitter tears of lives I'd ruined with a pink slip.[1]

With nowhere in particular to be, I meandered, crossing Clark Street at the light to reach a small city park with maple trees that wouldn't reach maturity in this century, a little playground with a sun shade, and a recycled rubber tire running track that crossed through the limited greenspace like a drunken snake trying to bite its own tail.

---

[1] Technically this is a lie. Dulcie Waterhouse ruined her own life by embezzling from her firm and taking too many long lunch breaks buying macarons across town. The only tears were the tears of joy in her co-workers' eyes when they realized she was leaving for good. And there wasn't a pink slip. I convinced her to resign. I'm good like that.

It was too early for school to be out and too late for lunch, which meant the park was populated by a muddy handful of toddlers, their attendant adults, and me. I kept to the outside track, crossing a stone footbridge over a shallow dirt ditch that might become a small pond if it rained. Tulips bobbed in the wind. The forsythia was out.

Little flowers and cheeky sparrows.

I enjoyed it for about four minutes before I could feel my brain scrabbling around like a trapped rat desperate for escape.

Natural vistas had that effect on me. I needed something to think about. A job to focus on. Numbers. Problems. City things.

At the sound of a jogger approaching, I stepped to the side so they could sweep past and catch the running track.

And sweep past he did. A gloriously muscular runner with olive-toned tan skin, a shock of silver-white hair shaved on the sides and long on top, a well-defined back and legs, and a black shirt sliding out of his waistband and dropping to the ground.

Well then.

It wasn't quite the young Miss Bennet dropping her gloves so a militia man could retrieve them for her, but it was possibly the twenty-first century equivalent. Even if it wasn't, it was only polite to collect the handsome man's shirt and return it to him.

I picked it up, shook off the dust and grass clippings, and held the sandalwood-scented shirt up for inspection. The owner was broad shouldered and the shirt was lean cut, meant to hug him and give everyone looking an excellent view of his well-defined muscles. Slightly more interesting was the word KILLER written across the front of the shirt in the font of the well-known horror brand, Slasher.

The jogger was a scary movie fan.

Not a lot to work with as openings went.

Scary movies weren't my cup of cocoa. No movies were, most days. Sitting still for hours on end listening to other people talk made me restless.

Perhaps it wasn't meant to be.

I folded the shirt neatly, and when I looked up the jogger was watching me from the bend of the running track only a few feet away, one white earbud hanging off his shoulder, the other still in his ear. He was younger than the white hair suggested, maybe twenties or early thirties, with dark brown—nearly black—eyes, high cheekbones, a well-defined jaw line, and a sharp, straight nose. He looked exceptionally in-tense and unquantifiably captivating.

"Is that my shirt?" he asked in a deep voice as delicious as he was. I could listen to that man read the dictionary and I'd love every moment of it.

I held the shirt up, letting it unfurl over my dress. "I don't know, do you think it's mine?" I let him get a good look at me. Large, dark reds curls that looked a century out of date, a pink flower tucked behind my ear, pink lipstick, pretty smile, A-line green dress with pink flowers embroidered on it and a crinoline underneath for volume; I looked like a piece of walking history.

Twee. Sweet. Friendly.

Stupid.

I'd heard every verdict, but the dress made me look fabulous and I loved bringing a pop of cheer to people's otherwise blighted lives.

"It'd look good on you. Killer." The corner of his mouth lifted in a sexy smile.

Oh. *No*. I did *not* like that.

Actually, I did, very much, but I knew where sexy smiles led. It would be hot nightclubs, wild parties, and then a trip to the suburbs as Mr. Sexy waxed lyrical about 'getting away from the city.' Pretty soon he'd be browsing baby name websites and talking about getting a dog.

No. If a *Timberwolf Town*[2] werewolf couldn't tempt me, then a yappy little dog suitable for the suburbs didn't stand a chance.

I held the shirt to my shoulders and tried not to notice how good it smelled—sandalwood with an undertone of mint. The scent was too light for a cologne—probably a soap. "It looks like my size, too." Assuming it was supposed to be worn halfway to my knees. Jogging, dark, and handsome was also tall, dark, and handsome.

"I'll let you borrow it some time." The man had dark, hungry eyes that promised to make my flirtation worth my time.

---

[2] A paranormal-horror series from the mid 20s that centered around a hidden werewolf population and their unrivaled basketball team. I'm 90% certain that the ratings were due to the regular shower scenes.

"Sure." That was never going to happen. I tossed the shirt to him. "Enjoy your run."

The smile turned to a smirk. "Enjoy the view." He secured the shirt to his waistband again and took off with a wink.

Confidence was always sexy, and I was very tempted to continue my little stroll around the park and see if the jogger wanted to join me for a post-workout snack somewhere.

I was great at first dates. Lots of confidence and a big smile got me everything I wanted.

Second dates?

No one had tempted me enough to schedule a second date since college.

I glanced at the jogger again. *Maybe* no one had tempted me?

He looked familiar in that we–met–once–in–passing sort of way.

My memory for names and faces was legendary, but I couldn't recall being introduced to him before.

It was going to bother me all afternoon if I didn't pursue it.

As if the office had a psychic link,[3] my phone rang, the quick staccato tattoo reserved for my boss. Work was there again, to rescue me from my worst impulses and save me from the kind of heartbreak ice cream couldn't fix.

---

[3] Or, let's be honest, a stopwatch to keep track of the betting on the Dulcie Waterhouse situation.

"Hi, Amara." I moved toward the crosswalk, dodging a little green car that nearly swerved into me. Chicago drivers. So charming.

There was a tiny community garden space across the street, a safe distance from the sexy jogger.

"Merri, I just heard the good word from Windy City Security, you've officially slayed the wicked witch of the upper west side. Did you break seven minutes?" Amara Rosa Park[4] was just as competitive as I was and she'd had my back in the office betting pool.

Sloan and Markham is *the* name in corporate accounting in Illinois. Amara is the head of the forensic accounting unit.

Really, we're a bunch of math nerds who read too many mystery novels and decided we'd grow up to fight white collar crime for a six-figure annual salary. And in the land of the nerds, I'm the big, brutal boss, the final, unconquerable hurdle.

"Six minutes," I said with a killer smile.[5]

"You make me so happy! Did Dulcie cry? I met her when I went in for the initial contact and..." Amara sighed. "Some people just *look* evil, you know?"

I pictured Dulcie Waterhouse in her gray pantsuit with a black silk shell under the jacket, two silver studs in each ear, a professional, asymmetrical cut for her dark brown hair, and dark red lipstick on a mouth pouring out more cuss words than could fit into a Monday morning commute when the trains were down. "She

---

[4] Named for Amara Enyia and Rosa Parks, obviously.
[5] Ha ha, I'm so funny!

didn't cry, but you may need to give the interns a bonus for reading my emails for the next few weeks."

"More death threats?" Amara sighed again. "What is it about you that attracts so much venom?"

"It's the job." And the fact that dressing like the lead singer from a retro throwback band made everyone underestimate me. What can I say? I have brains *and* beauty.

With a click of her tongue, Amara dismissed the disappointing news. "Well, done is done. I'll give the interns a heads up." There was a chime in the background. "Oh, and there's the first hit on social media. Want to hear it?"

"It's not like I'm going to look it up." I didn't do social media. Despite having an email assigned to me along with my social security number, I had the digital footprint of a ghost.

"The headline is 'Chicago's Infamous Grim Reaper Strikes Again.' Good job."

"I try my best."

Amara made a happy, purring sound. "Did you try your very best with Harry?"

"Harry?" I stopped in front of a bench. "I'm drawing a blank."

"Junior executive in accounting?" Amara dangled the tidbit.

Mentally I flipped through a detailed list of junior accounting people. "Not ringing any bells."

"Henderson account?"

I shuddered.

"He sent you a gorgeous bouquet of day lilies—"

"He was telling me about how his parents were building a new house in Sugar Grove and how the commute was under thirty minutes to the city with the new high-speed trains."

There was a stunned silence and then Amara took a deep breath. "So…"

"So, thanks but no thanks? Give them to someone else."

"He left a note too."

Stupid man. But it was only polite to read the note and find some excuse for why I couldn't show up to Domestication Of The Wild Wifey 101. "Leave it on my desk. I'll deal with it when I get back to the office."

"About that…."

"You have another job for me before the weekend?" If there were gods who smiled fondly on math nerds, I would have prayed. Numbers and patterns were my favorite candy. A weekend sorting through someone else's finances as just as blissful as a bubble bath.

There was a hesitant little sigh, which meant Amara wasn't sold on the job but someone was begging. "This is an odd one. It's not the bosses calling, it's an employee, and she asked for you by name because she said you worked here, but she didn't seem to know what it is you do."

Weird. "The name?"

"Ellen Berry."

Someone else would have a hazy memory of a schoolyard friend who they'd met during a game of tag-turned-head-on-collision in kindergarten. My memory was sharper than that, and off the top of my head I could rattle off all the major life events in Ellen's personal history up until she left for college in New York. We hadn't kept in touch mostly because I forgot people existed when I was working with math.

It was great for my bank account, but not for relationships.

"Merri?" Amara waited. "If I give you the address can you go over and see what's going on?"

"Sure. Where am I headed?"

"Cozy Studios—"

"Cozy as in Cozy TV with the candy-dipped romances?" Good grief. "Can I fire the writers for their poor plotlines?"

"Only if they're embezzling," Amara said. "Otherwise, give them the quick two-day special. A little workflow advice. A little hiring advice. And then get out of there, because we have the Oretega account to tackle next week."

Easy as mud pie in Mississippi. "Got it. In. Out. Tear-free."

"If you make it tear-free, I will personally buy you dinner anywhere in the city."

"I like expensive food," I warned.

"Cozy was just bought out by Slasher Corp," Amara reported with maybe just a soupçon of glee. "You're getting called in because Cozy is getting killed."

⌐

Cozy TV was on Goose Island at the corner of Hooker and Weed.[6] The place had gone through many changes over the decades. There'd been a research park there at the turn of the twenty-first century, a Wild Mile nature reserve that was abandoned during the recession in the twenties, and it was temporarily a swamp before the canals and dams regulated water levels in the thirties.

The original studio belonged to Whole Sum Entertainment, purveyors of movies and streaming videos for kids of all ages.

On the ride over I had one of the office minions read me the history. Whole Sum had broken up in the mid-thirties when the original owner was diagnosed with cancer. She broke it into pieces, creating Cozy TV, Chicago Tots,[7] Natural Adventures,[8] and the Whole Sum Learning Channel that featured streaming classes for everything from English basics to college-level science.

Whole Sum Learning went completely digital and was now a subscriber-based, nationally accredited online school for ages four and up. One of the new hires

---

[6] Yes, I did text my sister as soon as I saw the address. She teaches high school French and needs something other than eighty *"un ouef"* jokes to giggle over. Besides, there's a French connection between eighty and weed.
[7] And clothing line of the same name.
[8] Much to the entire office's surprise, this was about animals and not the Whole Sum porno department. With that name though…

at Sloan and Markham actually had gotten her degree from there. Overall, it was successful.

Chicago Tots kept the clothesline but partnered with an international studio. Nothing was left of them but the name.

Natural Adventures had fallen prey to Darwin's Law of survival of the fittest, becoming no more than a blip on the radar.

Cozy TV kept the studio space and survived on a steady diet of cozy shows. Everything from friendly-friendly travel adventures to cooking shows, to politicslite, to their internationally known holiday romances for all occasions.

Feeling like a St. Patrick's Day romcom? *Galloway Girl's Night Out.*

A feel-good Fourth of July romance? *For Love And Freedom.*

World Baking Day? *Bun In The Oven.*

Over the years they'd earned a comfortable profit, nothing too ostentatious, but certainly enough to keep them growing—until they hit an unexpected snag four years ago with no real explanation.

"Nothing?" I asked Willow Maguire, my team's go-to research person.

Over the car's speaker I could almost hear her shaking her head and adjusting the gold-rimmed glasses she wore for aesthetics. "There's nothing big. No major industry shifts. The only thing is that there was a rumor of an internal problem with the direction of their big holiday movie, *Mistletoe Mischief.*"

I crossed the bridge over North Branch Canal and turned onto Hooker Street. "What did you dig up on Slasher?"

"Nothing you probably didn't know," Willow said. "They're the Little Indie House That Could. Lots of low-budget horror movies, usually short, mostly streaming until two years ago. But they get rave reviews for the quality. Seth Morana is the CEO, lead creative director, art director, writer, and sometimes actor. His first movie to go to Sundance was a student film he wrote, directed, and acted in. But he was in a couple of big-budget movies too. *Scarred* and *Unforgiven?*"

The posters had been basic horror movie ads: black, white, gray, and a splash of blood red. *Scarred* had a hot-as-hell man looking away with six bloody scars on the side of an otherwise-flawless torso. *Unforgiven* had a sharp-nosed man with burning black eyes glaring directly at the viewer. I'd never watched either movie, but the reviews from my horror-loving friends were positive.

Another image flicked across my mind: dark eyes and dark hair with a chiseled jawline and a university sweatshirt. "Was he in *Timberwolf Town* too?"

"Checking," Willow said. There was the sound of clicking and then a small laugh. "As always, your memory is excellent. The year *Unforgiven* came out, Morana had a cameo in the last season of *Timberwolf Town*."

"So, we have one over-achieving horror geek. One romcom studio in need of revival. And one childhood best friend asking me to somehow save her from the serial killer."

"But what will you do after tea time?" Willow asked.

I turned into a gravel parking lot behind some dull gray sheds that looked like they'd started life as industrial warehouses, and sighed. "I'm here. If I don't check in by six, assume the serial killer from Studio B caught me."

"Best of luck, boss." Willow hung up.

It wasn't that I didn't want to help Ellen, honestly, but I wasn't sure there was anything I could do. I was a forensic accountant. What I knew about directing and producing movies had been learned off a quick internet search and one too many reruns of *Out Of The Spotlight* playing in the background during late-night number-crunching sessions.

The sale had been legal, my team would have spotted it otherwise. Really, the best I could offer at this point was a sympathetic ear.

Still... Cozy on the corner of Hooker and Weed? I was going be snort-giggling over that for weeks. Someone should have petitioned the city to change the name.

As I parked, I realized there was one more thing I should have asked Willow about: how to reach Ellen.

I suppose the office assumed that anyone asking for me by name had already talked to me and given me their contact information, but that's not how it worked in the rural Midwest.

Ellen had probably called her mother, who then went to talk to her neighbor, who went to church with my aunt, who saw my parents at Sunday night dinner, who remembered Little Ellen Berry who was so sweet and kind, and then they called mom's friend, who gave them the number for Mrs. Berry who then passed my work number to Ellen who then had an assistant call my office.

It was the small town phone tree, no social media required.

And while I could call the office and have them call Ellen while I waited for her, there was something nice about having the element of surprise. Walking into an office looking like the cheerful temp who's going to be answering the phones all day is a good way of measuring people. Time and again I'd learned that everyone treated me differently once they realized what my job was. It was a basic self-preservation skill.

City. Jungle. Et cetera, et cetera, et cetera.

I was the well-camouflaged hunter, like an orchid mantis or one of those deep-sea angler fish that looked like a friendly light in the darkness giving hope and joy to everyone right before the fangs closed around them. *Nom nom nom.*

Grinning at my reflection, I gave my strawberry-pink lipstick one more touch up and headed out to find Ellen Berry and the Cozy studios.

The building to the left of the parking lot looked grim, with darkly tinted solar windows[9] and no signage. To the right was a warehouse, the smell of second-rate catering, and the steady hum of machinery and noise. A narrow, dirt path led between a wooden fence and the warehouse; I followed it right into Winter Wonderland.

----

[9] The kind that replaced solar panels in most of Chicago several decades ago.

Literally.

There was a broken, wooden sign with distressed pink lettering and a beheaded elf.

There was also a sticky puddle of red that smelled like corn syrup and was probably fake blood. Probably not a Cozy set.

Carefully avoiding the puddle, I kept right, heading slowly toward the warehouse and the sound of voices muted by the scream of the dying ventilation unit.

I don't know what I actually expected to find. My ideas about Hollywood lots in general were all formed by repeated viewing of *Backlot* and *Ultra,* both shows set in pre-reform Hollywood, California, before the monopolies were broken up in the thirties.

Both shows left me with the impression that movie making was a huge undertaking, with a crew of hundreds and sets that could cover whole counties. That wasn't what I was seeing as I walked through Cozy's backlot. It was more like walking through a series of pocket dimensions. Little universes contained by thick, sound-dampening curtains, three sides of thin walls and a ceiling of light reflectors.

When I entered the sound stage in the warehouse, I saw huge overhead camera setups, lights, and larger sets that ranged from Mistletoe, Minnesota,[10] to a fake beach complete with a shallow pool of water in front of a green screen. Each set had a huddle of people, most wearing jeans or shorts paired with a jokeish holiday t-

---

[10] Home of the *Mistletoe Kisses* series that made Cozy so popular.

shirt, and then heavily made-up, heavily perspiring actors bundled in winter coats, despite the spring weather outside.

"If you take another step, I'm going to have to kiss you."

"What?" I spun fast enough to make my skirt flare.

A sandy-haired man with sparkling blue eyes and the biceps of a dedicated gym aficionado smiled back at me. His grimy, once-white t-shirt had a picture of a body building Santa and the words 'Santa Stud', so I figured he belonged to Cozy. "Hi," he said.

"Hello." I put enough ice into the greeting to create a polar vortex.

"You've got to watch out for the mistletoe." He gestured above our heads.

"Thanks. I'll keep that in mind." I took a deliberate step to the left without looking up.

"I'm Noah, by the way." Sexy Santa held out a strong, tanned, calloused hand. "I do set design."

I ignored it. "I'm just passing through."

"Right..." His eyes dragged down and back up. "Cute costume. Do you work for Slasher?"

"Do I look like I work for Slasher?"

Again, he looked me up and down, appreciation in his eyes. "You look like you could keep a man up at night."

I smiled. "Thank you for the compliment."

"Any time, beautiful."

"Lesbians!" someone screamed behind me.

I turned in time to see a trim, bald man wearing pink sunglasses, a black sweater, black shorts and waving an actual clipboard with paper in the air.

A woman with short, curled gray hair and purple t-shirt with a kitten in a Santa hat ran up to him. "Have you seen the mistletoe bouquet?"

"Nope," the man in pink glasses said, "no bouquets. I'm zombie wrangling."

"Noah?"

"Sorry, Bee." Santa Stud shook his head.

She nodded and rushed off.

The bald man took a deep breath and shouted, "Lesbians! Where are the lesbians?"

Noah winked at me as he sauntered off.

A pair of women in matching bridal gowns ran up, one with shaggy, blonde hair with the tips dyed an atrocious mildew green that clashed with her too-pale skin. The other looked like she was ready to play Okoye in the reboot of the *Black Panther* movies. She waved at the man. "We're the lesbians!"

He checked his clipboard. "Ghosts or zombies?"

"Mistletoe Miss," the blonde said.

"Wrong lesbians!" He marched away, clearly enraged that the lovely ladies were not undead.

They glanced at each other, shrugged, and then looked at me.

"Are you looking for lesbians?" the blonde asked.

"I'm looking for Ellen Berry," I said, "but I have a sister who likes lesbians." I reached for my purse where I kept a couple of Lucky's business cards for just such occasions, but the second lesbian shook her head.

"We're already—" She waved a hand between herself and her co-star. "On set romance."

"Cozy Curse!" the blonde said cheerfully, shaking her silk flower bouquet at me and hugging her wife-to-be's arm.

I nodded. "Understood. Congratulations."

"Thanks!"

The future general of Wakanda pointed down the row of lights. "Ellen is over in Paradise, I think."

"Thank you."

Off in the distance, someone called for the kissing misses and the brides rushed off to Montana waving and running much better than I ever could on matching high heels.

Paradise… Hopefully that was a set and I wasn't interrupting a private moment between Ellen and who-ever she was with these days. She hadn't dated in high school, and I couldn't remember anyone mentioning her with a partner in college.

I knew for a fact she wasn't married because that kind of news would have reached me even if I were on the moon. But maybe it wasn't news she was sharing yet.

I walked through wintery scenes, gazebos and pine forests, and coffee shops, and remote cabins.[11] Snow really is prettier when it isn't cold enough to freeze your nose off outside. Cozy's brand managed to encapsulate my two least favorite things: winter holidays and small towns.

No one truly understands how horrible Christmas can be until they have to have a mock cheese made of

---

[11] With only one bed! Oh my!

fish and almonds, or locally-sourced beaver tail, with a group of random grad students who showed up for a three-week intensive course on twelfth century English history.

One time is fun. Getting a slightly moldy orange and two pence every Christmas for eighteen years while your parents spend their time with guests and your sister goes to winter training camp is significantly less fun.

Sure, I'm fluent in Middle English, but I really prefer summer holidays. It's hard to go wrong with fireworks and barbecue.

"Merri?" The voice of my childhood friend had gotten richer over the years, like a fine wine, but I knew Ellen's voice anywhere.

I pivoted in a swirl of skirt. "Ellen!"

"Aahh!" Ellen looked the same as she had at graduation: curly black hair cut to shoulder length, a galaxy of dark freckles across her permanently and perfectly tanned, cider-brown skin, bright gray eyes, and a wide smile. She wore a shell-pink blazer, champagne satin camisole, and a cute pencil skirt. "Merri! You made it!" She wrapped me in an enthusiastic hug.

I had a height advantage only because I was wearing two-inch heels. Ellen had the muscle advantage of being the former state wrestling champion for her weight class—women's and co-ed—from ninth grade through college graduation. "Can't breathe! Can't breathe! You are squishing me!"

She gave me one more tight squeeze and released me back like a little kid releasing a goldfish they just tried to kiss. Her smile was even brighter than mine. "I didn't think you'd come!"

"For you? I'd drop anything," I promised. Linking arms with her, I walked away from the movie sets smelling of pine wood and fake snow, back to the garish light of day.[12] "So, tell me every little thing. Why'd you need to see me at work and not for brunch?"

"All I want from Kriesmas is for her to play grim reaper and kill some problems for me."

"Done," I promised. "Tell me where to start."

"First, because I didn't even realize we were in the same city," Ellen said as she led me to a park bench under a small, fake maple tree with silk leaves glued to the branches and nailed to the ground. "Your digital footprint is nonexistent."

"That's intentional," I assured her. "I get stalkers. I get haters. I get death threats. I am the Grinchiest Woman In America according to a recent poll and—at last count—there were seventy-two public videos where my face has been imposed over Scrooge's in various iterations of Dicken's classic *A Christmas Carol*. Thankfully it's the slightly blurred photo from the newspapers, but still, I'm not putting any of my social life out on the internet. Also," I added, "I don't have a social life. I have work."

"Sounds like me," Ellen said sympathetically. She sat next to me on the bench. When she saw my dubious expression, she giggled. "This is the set for the save-

---

[12] So bright. So imperfect. So obviously not filtered to make skin look poreless.

the-date promo photos we're doing for most our movies. Right now *all* the outside sets are for promo shots to share on social media. They're mostly wedding invite-themed."

I nodded. "Even Winter Wonderland?"

"*Holiday of Horrors* for Slasher." Her mouth twisted at the name and her shoulders hunched forward.

"Is Slasher really that bad?"

"For a bunch of Goth Gremlins who get their wiggles and giggles out of watching serial killers?" she asked with a stretched tone. "No. They're fine. I mean, they're polite at least. I haven't heard any of them actually making fun of Cozy." She named the studio like it was her precious puppy or only child. "But they give us looks and…." She sighed heavily. "I mean, it's obvious what they're doing, right? There's no way Seth Morana is going to keep Cozy going. The only reason we're still kicking is because there are contracts Morana couldn't get out of."

"Has he told you that?"

Ellen shook her head, tight curls moving as a unit. "No, the amount of senior staff abandoning Cozy around the time of sale told me that. Merri, I was hired last year as a costumer. That's it. Now I'm basically running the production of all the Cozy movies. I'm on the Slasher executive board, officially. That doesn't happen in healthy companies."

"Transitions can be rough," I said.

There wasn't much information to go on, but mass quittings after a change of ownership weren't necessarily a red flag for me. "I'm sure you can handle this."

"I'm sure I can't," Ellen said glumly. She leaned against the back of the bench with a sigh as someone in the distance yelled for mistletoe. "We had a policy to pay up front for as much as possible. Everything from salaries to the marketing budget is set aside before filming starts and stays there. In January I was told it was all there, the full Cozy budget. I want to start paying and…" She shook her head as she stared out at the fake, brown grass. "I can't."

"Was it stolen?"

She shook her head again. "Each quarter's budget is sectioned off, there's some accounting magic the CFO does." She waved her hand to scare off a passing dragonfly that had found its way into the set warehouse. "I accessed the second quarter budget this week, after I got my new computer, and it's not enough. Morana said this was the same budget Cozy had used for the past three years. It was the projected budget for this year, including our big, new movie."

I looked at her with interest. "I thought all the movies were new?"

"About forty percent," Ellen said, easily falling into the stats because she'd always been good with them. "We show a mix of past favorites, ones we loved but that didn't get enough public love, and then our new ones. But *A Midwinter Wish* is a totally different style than anything Cozy's done before. It's an interactive holiday romance. The heroine wishes for love on a shooting star on the night of the winter solstice, and when she wishes the star breaks into three pieces. It's technically difficult because we have to set up all three romances. And it's more expensive to film, and post-production tripled and so did marketing. It's a great idea, but really ambitious and very expensive. Very, very expensive." Ellen glanced up at me guiltily, then went back to studying the impaled leaf as if spending money was a sin.

"And the budget doesn't cover it?"

She reached for the pocket of her shell-pink blazer and pulled out a folded, multi-creased piece of paper that had obviously been crumpled, tossed away, retrieved, smoothed, and refolded.

I unfolded it and looked at the number. "Fifteen thousand? How much does it take to make most your movies?"

"The cheap ones run fifty thousand, and that's with no-name actors reusing sets. Bigger projects usually run close to a hundred thousand, and that's after accounting for the product placement and ad revenue. Subscriptions help, but where we really make money is having the sales. Every piece of wardrobe is available on our website. You see a toy? You can buy it through Cozy. We team up with every major brand in thirty-four countries."

"But fifteen thousand—"

"—doesn't buy me anything." She nodded. "It'll cover a half a week of wages for a full crew or, maybe, a few cheap dinners for everyone."

"What did Morana say?"

"That he checked the numbers and he thinks that the budget is enough. If I need more, we can talk about it at the next meeting. But, I have to pay people now.

Patrick Miles is supposed to be flying in tonight to start filming his portion. If I don't have the money for him, he's going to be on the red-eye back to Portland. As for everyone else? I have less than two weeks to make this money magically appear." She looked ready to cry.

Patrick Miles was Ellen's celebrity crush. Missing a chance to meet him because of a budget mishap would…

Okay… it wouldn't be the end of the world. But Ellen would be sad, and I could never let that happen.

I refolded the paper as I thought. "Do you think this is the budget Cozy had before?"

"Absolutely not." Ellen was confident. "I started working budgets last summer. I know this isn't what we spent."

"Have you talked to Morana face to face?"

Ellen suddenly became very interested in one of the fake, orange leaves nailed to the fake, brown grass.

"You didn't," I said flatly.

"He's hard to find!" Ellen protested. "And he's scary. He creeps me out."

My eyes narrowed immediately. The chances that I would let Seth Morana scare my best friend were about as good as me retiring to North Pole, Alaska, or re-leasing an album of Christmas carols.

"No!" She held up her hands to keep me from mur-dering her creepy boss. "Not, like, he's done anything creepy. He's just so quiet, and he just stares at you until you start to ramble. I don't like dealing with him. I don't like dealing with anyone from Slasher," she ad-mitted. "They all have awards and experience and I feel like an idiot. They're polite, but, you know how it is when people just stare at you?"

She wilted like a rose at the first touch of frost.

Ellen had never been particularly good with confrontation. It's part of the reason we were best friends: my sister and I were very good at confrontation of every kind. That, and after bumping heads on the playground Ellen had spent a week following me around apologizing. I'd finally convinced her she wasn't supposed to say sorry because bumping heads made us best friends. It'd sorta been a lie at the time, but it worked out and became a self-fulfilling prophecy.

She was overwhelmed, she felt unskilled, she felt like she was letting everyone down, so she'd reached out. That made perfect sense. To me.

I patted her arm. "Do you have the account books?"

"Yes." Ellen sniffled a little. "But they're old school."

"What? Like… Excel? OpenOffice?"

"Pen and paper."

I stared at her in horror. "Ellen, that's not funny."

"I know. I have an entire office full of brown boxes of pen and paper accountant ledgers and checkbooks with pre-signed checks."

My stomach turned and I felt faint. "That's… that's not even legal! To sell Cozy they had to have digital accounts."

"Morana might have those," Ellen said. "I don't."

"Right." I stood up, brushing off sawdust from my skirt. "Then step one is to track down the serial killer CEO and get the digital records from him."

"Can you do that?"

I thought about it. "Are you officially asking me to do an audit and performance review of Cozy Studios?"

She looked up at me, gray eyes wide, waiting for a hint.

I nodded.

Ellen nodded.

"Then, yes, legally you are allowed to ask for an audit and I am allowed to request the records for the audit, unless Morana did something very sketchy during the sale."

"I probably can't pay you your regular rate."

"True. That's why I'm charging you the friends and family rate: you owe me a meal."

Ellen jumped up and hugged me. "You're the best!"

"I know." I managed to wiggle loose of her grasp again. Barely. "Where can I find tall, dark, and dangerous?"

She jerked a thumb in the direction of the building I'd avoided. "Slasher HQ. Lurking somewhere."

"Grand." I nodded as I mentally lined up my arguments. "Is there anything else I should know?"

Ellen frowned and then shook her head. "It's pretty simple. I need a bigger budget or the miracle of everyone volunteering everything."

"What's the Cozy Curse?"

She froze, a deer in the headlights caught robbing the bank. "Um..."

"Ellen Petunia Berry!" I put a lot of menace into those eight syllables.

"It's a joke!" she bleated out. "Sort of. It's, it's this thing. Superstition, that before the filming wraps on the big holiday movie of the year everyone who's single will be with someone special."

I might have stepped back.

Not saying I did.

I'm in no way suggesting I was reacting like Ellen said she had a mutated super-form of the Ebola virus. But I may have stepped away from her and a little closer to Slasher's Winter Wonderland of horrors set for absolutely no discernible reason at all.

"Really, it's just the natural outcome of single, attractive people working on romances and sweet, family-friendly holiday movies for every kind of family." I was impressed that Ellen could get the studio slogan into a panicked ramble. "It's not like you're single."

"Perpetually," I muttered.

"Or looking."

"Only sometimes." At joggers who lost their shirts in the park.

"And you won't be here very long."

"True." Monday morning, I'd be at Oretega no matter what.

"So you should be safe." Ellen hadn't made eye contact the whole time.

I *should* be safe?

Oh, dear, sweet, innocent Ellen. That was not how the world worked.

I was *always* safe. It was the rest of the world who needed to be protected from me. Especially best friends since kindergarten who weren't telling the whole truth.

Smirking, I crossed my arms. "Are you safe, Ellen?" I asked ever so sweetly.

Ellen didn't blush like some charming cartoon character with a little glow on her cheeks. No, Ellen's blush was a steadily rising color that scaled her neck, climbed across her nose, and turned the tips of her ears a blushing bronze. "There's no one," she lied like a liar.

I tried to stay angry, but wound up laughing. "How would Patrick Miles feel about being called No One?"

Ellen glare told me I'd gotten it right in one. She crossed her arms. "Merri! If you tell my mother—"

"I won't!" I promised. "But you have to tell me if anything happens! That's what best friends are for."

Her gaze dropped to the ground again and she shook her head. "It's—no—it's nothing. I had a bad break up before I moved back to Chicago and started working at Cozy. I'm not going to read things into it. I'm not… I'm not looking. It's just… Patrick Miles is coming. To film. In our big holiday movie."

"And he's single and you've had a crush on him since he was in the live-action remake of *Rescue Otters* when he was twelve.[13]" I nodded. "Do you want me to run a background check?"

"Merri!" Ellen's shriek sent a flock of birds into hurried flight, and someone on the other side of the set cursed. "Merri," Ellen said in a calmer tone. "No. It's

---

[13] Ellen dragged me to watch it in the outdoor theater sixteen times during the opening week. Six. Teen. I had seventy-three mosquito bites before Patrick's first on-screen kiss.

nothing. It's a silly, childhood crush. I'm just excited because…. Because." She nodded firmly. "When I have a relationship that becomes something, I will tell you."

"Hmm." I took out my business card and wrote my personal number next to the office number. "Fine. Keep your secrets. You still owe me dinner."

"Only if Morana actually lets you do the audit."

I smiled at her. "Ellen, my dear, this is me. I'm the Grim Reaper of Chicago. The Wicked Witch of the South Side. My job is auditing companies and making their numbers dance. And when I go talk to Morana, I'm going to turn on the tunes and see his budget twirl around a pole."

She covered her eyes. "Gargh! I just had a mental image of my boss pole dancing! Merri! Stop!"

"You want me to use a strip tease metaphor?"

If possible, she turned even redder.

I grinned.

"Go!" Ellen ordered between giggles. "Just… go!"

Me: 1

World: 0

I'd made my best friend laugh despite her circumstances, and now I was going to fix her problems, stubborn Slasher CEO or no.

The grey sheds on the other side of the lot, as it turned out, were mostly a huge props warehouse with a few shared sets waiting for stock footage filming, and an ominous grey building on the far side of the gravel lot that housed all the main offices.

That meant I had to walk through Cozy's winter wonderland—fake snow and small-town sets included—to reach my destination. Someone was playing Christmas music that made my teeth grind as I walked past a blonde bride in a huge white dress with layers of lace and rhinestones in a pile of fake mistletoe sprigs.

The whole set screamed.

Not screamed Christmas Romance or Holiday Wonder, just screamed, like the monster out of my worst nightmares chasing me over hill and dale.

Cozy's offices were the closest to the set—or I assumed they were Cozy's. Painted hearts and cartoon bluebirds lined the cheerful, rose-pink walls and the offices were filled with more white satin and canisters of fake snow than I ever wanted to imagine existed.

Heavy, industrial double-doors divided the Cozy workspace from a small reception area for Slasher. It couldn't be anything else. Black walls, black floor, black ceiling, black stairs with plexiglass rails, black–haircut–buzzed–short Black receptionist wearing all-black, standing behind a black counter with a blood-red neon sign carving out the word SLASHER in the now-familiar font. The only thing that didn't scream murder was the three gold stars painted along the receptionist's tight jawline as they ground their teeth.

With a sarcastic little smile, the receptionist turned their back on me and pulled out their phone. "Go back the way you came, princess. Cozy auditions are on the other side of the lot." It didn't sound mean, simply bored.

Maybe they had an allergy to colors.

The hallway ahead looked like it led to offices; probably movie HQ for all the chaos outside. Meeting the directors was certainly on someone's bucket list, but not mine. I wanted to go straight to the top.

And I didn't trust elevators in buildings older than me.

Sashaying past the receptionist, I took the black stairs, admiring how the shining black of the floor made it look like I was floating over the abyss. Whoever had done the interior design for Slasher had gone in for *Aesthetic* and I loved it for many reasons, not the least of which was that under the recessed spotlights I glowed like Persephone entering the Underworld.

Hopefully Hades was home.

As I ascended to the upper level, there was a sharp, staccato sound of stilettos snapping against the black tile.

A woman turned the corner, almost pushing me down the stairs. She was willowy and tall, with short-cropped neon-pink hair, black contacts with pink stars for pupils, and three silver rings pierced into her right eyebrow along with the Slasher uniform of all-black that hugged the tight, straight lines of her body.

Short nails too. Unpainted.

I wondered if she liked rugby.

But I didn't ask, because I've found that not every woman I meet wants me to start matchmaking as soon as I notice them. It was just that she was exactly Lucky's type.[14]

The pink-haired potential sister-in-law stopped short and glared at me. It was a good glare. She had at least eight inches on me and a face meant for brooding, withering scorn.

I smiled up at her.

She crossed her arms.

Out of the corner of my eye I saw movement—a figure wearing a black hoodie accessing the upstairs snack bar. So, we had an audience. I smiled brighter and pulled a business card out of my clutch to offer to the pink-haired Cerberus. "Merri Kriesmas."

"It's April."

"My name is still Merri Kriesmas in April." I wiggled the card a little.

"Alisson Baxter, CFO of Slasher." She unfolded, slowly reaching for my business card. After an obvious show of hesitation, she took it and read, just in case I was lying about my name. "Really? Kriesmas is pronounced Christmas?"

"It sure is." With my smile screwed in placed, I waited for the inevitable commentary.

---

[14] Her birth certificate says Carol Danvers Kriesmas but no one has called her that since the incident in Kindergarten that ended in five black eyes, a two-week suspension, and everyone agreeing that her name was Lucky. She plays rugby and does roller derby under the name Luck O' The Irish at night, and teaches French at a private school in the suburbs during the day.

"Your family must get wild around the holidays."

"Actually, we're Satanists, so the whole Christmas season is very bleak for us. Birth of the Destroyer of the Father of Lies—"

The person in the kitchenette spat their drink everywhere as they choked on a laugh.

"—It's a very hard thing to endure." I gave my curls a little toss so the fiery red caught the lights. "Don't worry. Taking my business card in no way contractually obligates you to be a human sacrifice at the first black mass you attend."

"And the second?"

Oh, I do love the smart ones. My smile widened. "I make no promises."

"Right." Alisson did her best to skewer me with a glare, but I was immune. "Why are you here? We didn't call Sloan and Markham."

"I'm here to steal something from your CEO."

It sounded like the person trying to enjoy their drink was going to die from the sputtering off to the side.

Alisson's face froze in a glower that would probably scare lions, tigers, bears, or men, but that couldn't find a chink in my armor. "What, exactly, do you intend to steal?"

"His soul," I said ominously, leaning ever so slightly forward.

My future sister-in-law backed up in an admirable show of self-preservation.

"Or his time, if that's available." I smiled. Alisson wasn't going to call Lucky if she was too scared. "Ellen Berry is an old friend of mine and she asked me to look over her new budget. A little confirmation about the details from Mister Morana will speed things along."

Alisson glanced over at the hooded figure. "Seth's over there. Ask him if he has time, and then get lost when he says no."

Ah, so our audience was also my target. That saved time. "I am certain Mister Morana will make time for me."

With a gesture that was a cross between Good Luck and It's Your Funeral, Alisson moved to step around me.

"Do you like rugby?" Ha ha. I was not letting her go that easy.

"What?"

"Rugby. Or roller derby?"

"Why?" she asked in a voice of mixed fascination and fear.

"My sister's single and she likes both." I pulled one of Lucky's business cards out and held it out to Alisson.

The deep red blush actually went very well with her pink hair. She snatched the card with undue haste and hurried down the stairs. See Spot run.[15]

Breaking into Hell was easy if you threw the guard dog a bone.

Time to go see Death.

Seth Morana was hiding behind a white mug with a black grim reaper and the words FINAL BOSS visible. How appropriate.

---

[15] I'll give you this as a freebie: Cerberus is Greek for Spot.

The Cozy Killer was a tall man. I couldn't see his expression—his face was hidden by the shadows of his black hoodie, the Slasher logo embroidered in metallic black thread blazing across his chest—but he hadn't run, so I took it as an invitation.

Pulling out another one of my business cards, I sauntered into the open dining area, heels clicking on the dark wooden floor. "Good afternoon."

"Merry Christmas." A strong, tan hand reached out for my card. "Oh, Meredith." His tone didn't give away his feelings on my full name.

"My mother is Mary with the traditional spelling," I offered helpfully. As ice breakers went, letting someone laugh about my name was easier than demanding they hand over their financial information. "My father is Holland, but he goes by Holly."

"And your sister?"

"Lucky."

"So they stopped the cruel naming trend after you?" He sipped what smelled like mint tea.

"No, her legal name is Carol, but you only call her that if you want facial reconstruction without anesthetic." I smiled. "Do you want to talk here or in your office?"

He sipped his tea again as a delaying tactic. "What if I want neither?"

"I'll rephrase: do you want to talk to me or the corporate lawyer who charges in ten minute increments?"

Morana tipped his head in acknowledgment. He walked past me and I saw a glint of dark eyes and pale hair under his hood. "Let's step into my office."

"Said the spider to the parasitic wasp."

He paused and turned to look at me again. "Don't you mean fly?"

"No, I mean parasitic wasp, as in genus *Acrotaphus*[16] that preys on innocent spiders." The brighter my smile, the more confused I made everyone around me. It was delightful.

Morana sipped some more tea as he made a puzzled 'hmmm' sound and led the way past various goth-stylized black doors to a space that had to be a door only because portals to blackholes didn't usually have air conditioning.

Everything from floor to ceiling was black, with dramatic spot lighting on the huge, curving black desk and the framed props hung as art. A silver scythe with delicate filigrees. A skull made of gold and bone that grinned forever at eternity. The infamous diamond-and-ruby heart from *The Dragon's Bride*.

Office décor said a lot about a person.

Cluttered desks meant an over-active mind or an overworked worker. Clean and sterile office spaces were common when someone was expecting to get fired, or interviewing with the competition. Morana's space was dark but comfortable. It was a space for someone who loved the horror genre to come and reflect on the triumphs.

"You have a nice collection," I murmured, walking under the lights and inspecting each piece. The room

---

[16] Did you want zombie spiders? This is how you get zombie spiders.

was chill, with the scent of mint and Morana's sandal-wood soap, the walls so dark they seemed to swallow the light, leaving nothing but pinpoint stars around the displayed treasures.

"Thank you." Morana sat behind his desk. "They aren't all from my movies, but they are all important."

"Mmm," I murmured in agreement as I stopped beside a wide-brimmed, low crowned black hat commonly worn by Grim Reapers in Korean shows. There was something written on it in silver in an alphabet I could recognize as Hangul but that I couldn't read.

Morana brushed his hood back, exposing a tan, chiseled face that was as beautiful as everything else in the room. A straight, pointed nose, high cheekbones, stunningly black eyes, and a shock of platinum hair styled in an I–just–had–wild–sex–and–came–to–work–smiling sort of way. "First you steal my shirt. Now you want my soul or my time. What's next, my heart?"

That's why he'd seemed familiar.

The jogger from earlier was the hottest actor in horror and the Slasher CEO.

It was easy to see why his movies, plot-poor though they'd been, had been so popular. He had a lean, hungry look and he watched me like a jackal, tracking my movements with dark eyes and a raised eyebrow.

I sat down across from him, smoothing my skirt with a slow, practiced movement.

His eyes stayed on my face.

"Tempting," I said. "One heart, like new, never been used."

Morana's lips pulled together as he tried to squelch a smile.

"But that presupposes that you had a heart to begin with."

"Are you saying I'm heartless?"

"Your business dealings certainly suggest it. Tell me, what are your intentions for Cozy?"

Morana settled back in his chair with a small smile. "My intentions? Are you Cozy's mother?"

"Only a concerned best friend."

"The kind who will leave my body in the woods if my intentions aren't pure?"

I smiled ever so sweetly. "Mister Morana, I would never be so crass."

He raised an eyebrow, a sexy smirk playing across his lips.

"If I killed you, I'd weigh your body down and dump you in Lake Michigan for the fish to nibble on. Only an amateur leaves bodies in the woods."

That made him crack. A gorgeous smile spread across his face with a warm laugh and a spark in his eye that made me want to lean in.

Hoo boy.

I was in trouble.

It had been a long time since I'd felt this kind of instant attraction. The last time had ended in tears—his, not mine—when I handed back the engagement ring and told him I'd never be the kind of girl he wanted.

I was never the kind of girl the boys wanted.

"Miss Kriesmas—"

"You can call me Merri."

"Only if you call me Seth." An outright challenge.

I smiled and tilted my chin up, acknowledging the possibility.

Seth nodded back. "My intentions for Cozy are honorable, I promise. We're in the same business."

"Horror and romance are the same business?"

He shrugged. "Horror takes something beautiful and familiar and makes it terrifying. It imagines the worst possible outcome of any situation. Romance takes the unknown and frightening and makes it beautiful. There's nothing more terrifying than falling in love. You never know if it will end in heartbreak or happiness.

"That moment of free fall, when you're racing between what was and what will be, is where Slasher and Cozy have a captive audience. We're both targeting viewers who want to feel something. They want us to toy with their emotions. To make them believe in ghosts and monsters, or magic and romance, even if it's only for a few hours."

"And you expect Cozy to do that with the budget they have?" I asked skeptically.

"It's a generous budget." Morana shrugged.

I narrowed my eyes. There was a fundamental disconnect here and I was missing something. "How much do your movies usually cost?"

"Ninety thousand apiece, on average. Some go over, a lot of sequels come in under budget because we can reuse footage and sets."

"But you don't expect anyone to make a big holiday movie with fifteen thousand."

He laughed again. "No! That's… that's low even for a student budget. Student movies are cheap because most of the work is done for free by students who use the production for a grade."

"So why is Ellen's budget fifteen thousand?"

The Slasher CEO stilled, staring at me with unblinking black eyes.

No. It didn't scare me. It made me want to smile in a way wholly inappropriate for the venue.

"Ellen's budget is significantly higher than that."

I pulled out Ellen's paperwork and handed it to Seth, being carefully not to let my fingertips brush his. "She printed this yesterday."

He frowned at it and then flipped part of the desktop up, opening a computer screen and keyboard. "That's not right at all." A few clicks and he turned the monitor to me. "This is Ellen's budget. A little over one million, five hundred thousand. It's everything that was in Cozy's account when I bought the studio."

"Then why doesn't she see this?"

"I don't know. It's the account I checked when she emailed me last week." Seth checked the account numbers, muttering under his breath. "Same account. Same bank. Her name is on here as authorized for access."

I smelled shenanigans. Standing slowly, I asked, "May I see your screen?"

Seth hit me with a territorial glare. "Miss—"

I raised an eyebrow in rebuke.

"Merri, I appreciate you coming out to the studio. I appreciate you stepping in and bringing this problem to my attention, but I can solve this in-house. Alisson is an amazing CFO and I'm confident she'll have it sorted by the end of the day. Slasher didn't hire Sloan and Markham and we don't need you here."

Right. Simple miscommunication. Ellen had logged into the wrong account. Or the wrong website. Or used the internet wrong, even though she'd been using it since infancy because her parents had one of those invasive Baby Needs! panels attached to her crib so she could poke at colored things like a lab rat requesting food.[17]

It was cute Morana thought I was going to give this up. "I'm sure Alisson is very competent. And I'm not auditioning for her job. I'm putting my expertise at your disposal."

"At a very high price." Trust the Slasher CEO to cut to the chase.

"For Ellen, the cost is a meal."

"You're working for free?"

"Pro bono." I smiled. "It's a slightly different tax code. Besides"—I sat back down—"I have the entire afternoon free. The whole weekend, in fact. Nothing happening until Monday morning, when I strut down to the Oretega Mineral Exchange to find out why their

---

[17] I hadn't been mad about it as a baby, but in fifth grade when we learned about the privacy wars of the twenties and thirties, I was absolutely furious anyone had been stupid enough to attach an uncontrolled camera to their infant's crib. Ellen had fond memories of her personal Big Brother spy-eye. I'd taken a baseball bat to my family's doorbell camera. We all coped with life differently.

sales numbers don't have the dazzling gleam they used to."

Seth's smile tightened with suppressed frustration. "Shouldn't you be doing something fun with your free time?"

"Math is fun."

"Math is fun enough that you'll work for me for free?"

I shrugged.

Most people would have been looking for a graceful exit. Seth leaned forward slightly as he uncrossed his arms.

He closed his eyes for a moment. Licked his lips. The look he gave me when he opened them was almost grateful, with only a touch of heat that could have been anger.

Or something else.

But it was probably anger.

"I'm not an idiot," Seth said. "Cozy was a good buy. Henry Lord wanted to retire, he'd been with Cozy since it was still part of Whole Sum Entertainment. They'd made decent money, but everything had plateaued. He thought *Mistletoe Mischief* was cursed. Trouble with props. Trouble with the set. Trouble with actors and contracts.

"I figured all Cozy needed was some fresh minds in the writers' room, a little infusion to get them up and running. Alisson and I checked everything. Multiple times. The company came to us clean."

Plateaus in sales were a red flag. Combined with the turnover Ellen had mentioned, I smelled a rat.

A long dead rat.

"It may have been clean because it was scrubbed," I said. "If that happened, I'm exactly who you need looking through the files. Give me a room with the paper records, access to the bank accounts, and I will find out what happened, why the sales went flat, and why Henry wanted to sell."

"In under three days?"

I nodded.

The corner of his mouth lifted in a smile. "Knock yourself dead, Killer."

"I'll never fall that far. I'm not that girl." I banged my head against my pillow and stared up at the ceiling. It was never a good sign when I had a Brutal Cheerleaders song stuck in my head at four in the morning.

After convincing Morana there was no harm in letting me sift through his budget, I'd spent the rest of the day doing archaeology work in the musty office where all the old records were kept. Some of them were still filed under Whole Sum, most were under Cozy, and all of them were dusty and erratic. The bookkeeping system seemed to change on a whim, and old files had never been updated.

Alisson had helped, checking the numbers on Ellen's computer against the paper records and the accounts Slasher could log into. She spent three hours on the phone with the bank, trying to figure out where the missing money was, only to discover that the account screen they saw didn't exist on the bank's server.

Words like Dummy Site, Cross Site Scripting, and Veiled Secondary Account escaped the conversation before Alisson stormed out of the room.

Ellen had brought us the leftover ham-and-cheese sandwiches from catering.

Noah, in his Santa Stud shirt, had brought us cookies and dropped his phone number off in case I needed him. I'd passed the number to Alisson, who passed it to Ellen, who passed it to the recycling bin.

Seth had dropped in a few times to whisper to Alisson and to give curious looks that turned to glares when I made eye contact.

It was almost midnight when Alisson had fallen asleep and we'd agreed to call it a night. I'd driven home as a storm rolled in over the lake, lightning dancing in the distance, but I couldn't sleep.

I'm not the woman in your dreams. I'm not the one holding on. My brain was stuck on a loop of numbers and music. Why—*Why?*—could I not let this go? Amara was right. This should have been an in-and-out fling with Cozy's accounts.

But I wasn't going to sleep until I figured out what my subconscious had caught that the rest of my brain had missed.

Having decided that, I tossed off the black comforter and padded through the shadows of my apartment by the light of the street lamp.

Turning on actual lights seemed superfluous: even with the lights on the furniture was black, white, and minimalist, with no stray anything. Ever. Clutter was not my aesthetic.

I pulled on a pink-and-black jogging suit with silver reflective strips, grabbed my gym bag, and ran the two miles to the gym along the quiet streets of Chicago as the winds picked up. This was the respectable end of town, which meant the all-night parties were in someone's penthouse suite, not on the street, and the security was unobtrusive.

Overhead, low storm clouds muttered in dissent.

My gym wasn't a fitness spa with low security and lots of cameras; it was the pricey gym in a high-end hotel that didn't ask names and had a very strict No Filming policy.

My freshman year of college, the specter of my very own porn movie—digitally created with footage of my soccer games—haunted my every move. It took seventeen months to take down because the people who can make digital revenge porn can also forge digital notes of consent. In the end, the judge took it down after my family's lawyer proved that some of the shots were of Lucky, who was under-age. But to get there I had to consent to a full-body shot presented in court to prove my freckles weren't my sister's.

It was one of the many reasons I kept my private life ultra-private.

I logged into the gym with a pin number, noted that there was one other person working out, locked my gear in a locker with another pin number, and dove into the lap pool to work my body while my brain turned over unconnected details.

Budget for props. *Lap.*

Accounting of lunches with staff. *Lap.*

Thank you gifts for TV talk shows hosts. *Lap.*

Increase of union dues. *Lap.*

Lap. Lap. Lap. Lap.

Someone else entered the gym wearing emerald-green swim trunks, but I ignored him.

Two accounts. *Lap.*

Money sloshing back and forth. *Lap.*

Money sloshing and going missing. *Lap.*

Where would the missing money go, though? It wasn't going to a shell company. No one was getting overpaid. I'd checked. Twice.

Lap. Lap. Lap.

I rolled in the water, kicking off the wall in frustration.

If I were a criminal wanting to siphon money from a studio, where would I put it? Tips? Paychecks? Props?

Lap. Lap.

Cozy sold replicas of everything in their shows, from the dresses to the furniture, and it was all appraised.

Appraisals could be faked.

Lap.

There had to be a third account.

I grabbed the wall as my thoughts churned. Holding my breath, I let myself sink down to the bottom of the thirty-foot pool.

A third account that caught the slosh when a prop was overvalued or overpaid for? That was sneaky. And not possible unless there was outside help.

Flexing my feet, I pushed toward the surface and hung off the wall again.

An operation like that would create a pattern not in money flow, but in types of payments around a transaction. And in trading partners.

If it were possible.

I sank back below the cold waters, letting the darkness steal away every distraction.

It was totally possible.

I needed to talk to Ellen.

I pulled myself out of the pool at the same time the other swimmer exited the far side.

He was a burly man who grabbed his green towel and water bottle in such a hurry that he dropped the bottle, sloshing it all over the tile floor.

As I dried myself off, I pretended not to notice the stranger's embarrassing distress. There were many reasons a person would come to this gym and wouldn't want to be noticed. And I respected all of them.

It would have been nice if the gentleman had come back to clean up the puddle, but what was more water on the floor around a pool? It was already spreading in front of the locker room doors, heading for the grates.

I ignored it and headed for the change rooms as my teeth started to chatter. It wasn't my concern.

Until it was.

I stepped forward and my foot kept going. Sliding. Slipping.

I tried to right myself.

Found both feet going forward on the now-slippery tiles as my head went back.

This was going to hurt.

Velocity of my steps.

Potential energy of height and weight.

Momentum—

Nothing.

I'd fallen against something hard, and warm, and…

My fingertips brushed over soft skin and muscular arms. I'd fallen into someone.

Panic pushed me to stand up, but whatever that man had spilled on the floor, I couldn't get any traction. I managed to twist around like a fawn on ice and fall right back into my rescuer's arms.

"Can I lift you up?"

"Sure," I said with a serious load of doubt seconds before the voice registered.

One of his arms went behind my back, the other swooped under my knees, and suddenly I was stunned silent and staring at Seth Morana, platinum hair damp from a shower—and missing a shirt.

Again.

I put my arms around his neck—just to help with the balance—and told myself not to stare. Heaven help me, but the man was hot enough to start another Great Chicago Fire.

Seth placed me on the metal bench by the door to the saunas and scooted away.

"Thanks." I managed not to sound too breathless. "You have exquisite timing."

"I saw a guy running through the locker room like the pool'd caught fire, so I thought I'd check to make sure no one needed help. I'm Red Cross certifi—" He glanced up at my face and he froze.

No-Makeup Merri… Yeah. Freckles, wide hips from a decidedly peasant heritage, ratty red hair tangled from swimming, bags under my eyes. No-Makeup Merri wasn't the kind of woman who drew appreciative looks from anyone. I waited with a polite smile for him to find an excuse to leave.

"Merri?" He looked me up and down in confusion, flashed his eyebrows up, and smiled at me. "I suddenly see why everyone else works out in the mornings. I usually don't get to the gym until after I wake up in the afternoons." Seth blinked and shook his head. "Sorry, I'm rambling. I didn't recognize you while you were swimming."

"That's fine," I said in a singsong voice. "No trouble at all. I'm fine now, so no harm no… concussion, I guess."

Honestly, the floors were hard enough that I probably would have had a very dramatic bleeding head wound if Seth hadn't saved me.

Best not to think about it. Or how I looked like the girl from the revenge porn.

I stared at the pool, focusing on the smell of chlorine as I waited for Seth to leave.

"Are you hurt?" Seth inched closer, as if I were going to fall apart.

"No." I turned back to him, waiting for the only-half-joking 'You Look Like A Girl I Know' that was always the opening line to asking if I'd ever filmed a sequel to *Saint Nick's Naughty List*.

Seth looked me up and down once, a small frown on his face. Then he scowled at the mysterious puddle. "What happened?"

I shrugged, refusing to look at him. "I don't know what happened. The other swimmer was hurrying to leave. He dropped his water bottle and it spilled, but he didn't have time to wipe it up. It must have been, uh…" Something. My brow furrowed.

It hadn't been water, but I couldn't think of another drink that slippery.

Seth dragged a finger along the bottom of my foot and rubbed it between his fingers. "Baby oil?"

"Why would someone have a water bottle filled with baby oil at the pool?" I demanded, annoyance making me turn to him.

A mischievous grin crossed Seth's face.

"A public pool," I reminded him with an eye roll. Reclaiming my foot, I started scrubbing off the oil with my towel.

"Maybe he wanted to get oiled up before he took a selfie." Seth managed to make a self-portrait sound salacious.

Or maybe I was projecting.

Seth was still sitting watching me with a half-smile and some very distracting abs.

"You can go," I said, projecting cheerfulness and pointedly not looking at his abs. At all. For which I should have been given an award. "Really. I'm fine."

"You say that, but I'm having trouble believing it."

"This isn't my first near-death experience."

Seth leaned forward conspiratorially. "If you wanted to flirt with death, I was right there all day. I'm a much better bang than the tile floor."

I held his gaze. "If I wanted to flirt with death, I would have winked in a mirror."

"I'd like to think I'm a better date than a mirror." Seth stood up and offered me his hand. "Ready to try walking again?"

"Sure!" His grip was gentle and sturdy, helping me stand on clean feet. "And look at that. I can stand again." I stepped away. "Thank you for saving me from a nasty headache."

"Any time." Seth stepped out of the way.

Forcing a cheerful smile, I went to the locker room, carefully avoiding the spill, and carefully not freaking out. Seth had to have noticed what I looked like. Had to have some opinion, at least. We were close in age[18] and any internet search with my name was going to pull up the super-fun trial, complete with commentary.

The only thing that knocked the trial off the front page of search results was the fact that I'd recommended firing a bunch of people on Christmas Eve last year.

I tried to slow my heartrate as I rinsed off. It was still dark out. I was supposed to be calming down, even though the sun would be up in an hour. I was also extroverted, which for me meant that being around a lot of people was like mainlining espressos. I needed

---

[18] Um, hello? Internet? Of course I looked up the stats on the hot guy I bumped into at work. You would too.

space away from people to calm down and to get my brain to shut up.

Swimming usually helped burn off the excess energy.

Slipping and winding up in Seth Morana's arms? Not so helpful.

As I whipped my hair into a braid, I glared at myself in the mirror.

Was I really going to let myself think about a relationship? Sure, Seth was exactly my type: fit, tall, dark eyes, light hair, muscles, and a quirky sense of humor. Oh, yeah, and he didn't back down.

But I had work.

I always had work.

Work was a beautiful, sturdy shield between me and Cupid's arrows of love. As long as Lucky kept getting lucky, my parents were content that at least one of their beloved children was headed to a life of marital bliss. That left me free to... not be on the path to a life of marital bliss and dying slowly in the suburbs.

I hadn't had a second date since college. And dating a guy whose company I was investigating?

Definitely off the table.

Most definitely.

Probably definitely.

Okay, I needed to stop thinking about Seth Morana and tables.

I zipped my jacket closed with more enthusiasm than strictly required. *Nope.* I was not being won over by dark eyes and sexy abs.

Grabbing my bag, I headed out, looking forward to renting a bike for a ride in the cool, early-morning air.

Seth was waiting by the check-in desk, wearing loose black pants and his oversized Slasher hoodie, casually leaning there and looking far too good for my peace of mind. "Merri." He tilted his head in the universally recognized gesture of 'Come Over Here'.

Reluctantly, I walked to him and the woman behind the counter. Her name tag said SYDNEY in blocky gold letters, and the yawn she was stifling said she wasn't a morning person.

"Good morning, miss," Sydney said without any pretense of perkiness. "We understand there was an incident in the gym this morning." Her voice was flat and her eyes slightly unfocused.

"There was a spill," I said, keeping my smile polite. I didn't expect anyone to be their best before 5am.

"We'll clean it up," Sydney said in a distant voice. "Would you like to file a report?"

Seth was watching the interplay like it was a Wimbledon match.

"No." I shook my head, more for Seth than for Sydney. "It's fine. Mop it up and call it a day."

"Yes, miss." Sydney yawned again.

"Have a good morning," I said, pivoting and heading for the elevator as fast as I could.

Seth caught up in a few long strides. And then stepped back when he saw my expression. "Should I wait for the next one?"

Yes, otherwise I'll be tempted to flirt with you.

"No. I don't mind sharing," I lied sweetly.

Seth stepped in and ran his tongue across his lips. "Want to share breakfast?"

Yes. I sighed. *And lunch. And dinner. Definitely dessert.* "No. I don't go home with people on the first date." And I should pretend I was going to go home and catch up on my missing sleep.

He winced playfully and pulled out his phone.

"Counting your rejections for the week?" I asked as the doors opened.

"Making a note to talk to Ellen." He slid his phone back into the pocket of his hoodie. "You don't know what a date is and that's something the Cozy crew should fix before you're done with your audit."

He did not... My eyes went wide as lighting cracked the sky, followed by rolling thunder. The storm had arrived. "You did not tell Ellen to set me up."

Seth shrugged as the elevator doors closed. "Got to do right by our favorite accountant." He winked at me. "Professional courtesy and all."

"This is revenge!" I pointed at him. "You're trying to get me sucked into the Cozy Curse! Saddle me with some third-rate actor who wants to settle in the sticks and raise cows."

"I do write horror," Seth said, as if that was any sort of explanation. "I know how this works. If I sacrifice you to the curse, I might be able to save myself."

"That decision will haunt you," I warned as the doors slid open again, revealing the beige-and-gold ground floor and a side exit near the bike racks.

Thunder roared ominously as rain pounded the ground.

Seth pulled car keys out of his pocket and pointed at the stairs. "You park downstairs or outside?"

"I jogged here."

He looked at the cold deluge outside. "You going to jog home?"

"I might wait in the lobby until the buses start running," I admitted with a grimace as I touched my hair.

"Worried about not being ready for your photo-shoot?" The question should have been teasing, but it sounded serious. He was trying to figure me out.

Thinking.

That could be dangerous.

I wasn't sure Seth would like what he found when he peeled away the colorful candy shell of my armor.

With a smile, I shrugged his question away. "I like controlling what people see. This isn't my usual day-wear." I gestured to my running outfit. "It's fine for a midnight workout but..." I wrinkled my nose. Maybe he got it. Maybe it didn't matter. My other options were letting a strange man drive me home—which was about as likely as me signing up for a lunar mission—or walking home in the rain. I wouldn't risk riding the city bikes in this weather.

"Like my hoodie?" Seth asked.

"Sure." I was focusing on the lobby and wondering where I could hide. "It'd look great on my floor."

Seth chuckled, and pulled his jacket off. He had a faded black t-shirt that clung to his biceps like a heart-sick fan.

I kind of envied the shirt.

He tossed me his hoodie.

I caught it on reflex and held it up.

"To wear, until you get back to… being comfortable or whatever."

"Thanks." *Awkward.* "Are you sure you can spare it?"

"I have more at home." He patted his pants pocket and grinned apologetically. "I do need my keys though. And my phone." He closed the distance between us and fished everything out of the pocket. "Feel free to toss this on your bedroom floor if you want." The whisper brushed my ear as he pulled away.

My cheeks warmed at the realization that I'd said that aloud. I shook my head, pretending it didn't happen. "It's good thing you're not famous enough to be followed by the paparazzi anymore. Early morning. A hotel."

"A mysterious, beautiful stranger?" Seth waggled his eyebrows at me. "Could be great publicity."

Danger! Danger! High levels of attraction detected!

"Shoo!"

Seth winked at me as he walked backward. "See ya later, Killer."

I rolled my eyes rather than dignifying that with a response. *Ridiculous flirt.*

I loved it. Not him, I promised myself, but I was always a fan of attention. And, Seth's hoodie? Soft, warm, and it smelled like clean soap and temptation.

Yeeaahhh… Seth wasn't getting this hoodie back.

It was oversized on him, but he was half a foot taller than me. The hoodie covered more of me than most of my dresses. I was going to spend the next hour curled up in a portable tent, enjoying whatever the hotel lobby had that passed for hot cocoa.

Maybe I wasn't the girl of anyone's dreams. And I wasn't holding on to some ephemeral hope for love from someone who understood me. But, every now and then, even the Grim Reaper of Chicago could have a good day.

Nine hours after being nearly knocked unconscious by a careless gym-goer, I was back on the sets of Cozy TV wearing a darling pink A-line dress with bright blue hydrangeas on it, red hair neatly tucked into shoulder-length retro pin curls, as I stood amid the mildew-scented hell of Mistletoe Lane counting props.

Cozy's aesthetic extended to their monstrous props warehouse.[19] One whole aisle was devoted to mistletoe: sprigs, balls, bouquets, clothes… If it involved mistletoe, it was here in a box or a bag or hanging from the ceiling far, far overhead. Not only did I feel shorter than usual next to the towering thirty-foot shelving units that looked like they'd been rescued from an abandoned Amazon warehouse, but there was a very real possibility that one of the gigantic vinyl snow globes would

---

[19] Now complete with real movie monsters, thanks to their relationship with Slasher.

spontaneously inflate, roll off the massive shelf, and crush me to death.

I eyed the mistletoe suspiciously. There was a monster movie in the making if all those little hemiparasitic plant balls ever became sentient.

The ones in the clear boxes near my head were mostly plastic, but the ones overhead were the custom jobs made of silk, gems, and crystals that glittered evilly under the industrial lighting. Windows would degrade the props, so even if it were a sunny day outside I'd be locked in the sinister gloom with the Ghost Of Winters Past. It was not a sunny day outside.

I checked the list on my phone as the thunder muttered outside. The lights overhead whimpered, screamed, and died. Again.

Under my breath, I counted to five, and nodded as the earthy curse of whatever poor soul was in charge of making sure Ellen had her lighting sounded.

Two thumps. Three. The generator rumbled to life and the lights overhead hummed as they considered turning on again.

Since I'd arrived, the same scene had repeated at least six times. Much to the dismay of Ellen, no doubt, who was currently on set with brown-haired, hazel-eyed Patrick Miles, former teenage heartthrob and current D-list actor looking to make a comeback after taking a sabbatical from the spotlight.

Patrick was only in Chicago for a week because someone was—in my opinion—terrible at scheduling around Chicago's spring weather. Just because it looked like I was stuck in a horror movie about possible small town Christmases did not mean it actually was December in the city.

Today was dedicated to lighting shots, promo shots, and the 'getting caught in the rain scene' that Ellen was so excited about.

Lightning turned the dark gray outside the giant, open doors of the warehouse to a blinding white, silhouetting a robed figure with a scythe.

The figure with the scythe was still there when the lights turned back on. Black pants, black hoodie, fake scythe, charming smile… Seth pulled his dripping hood back as he walked to the end of Mistletoe Lane. Smiling, he looked up at the threatening mass of holiday greenery. "You waiting for someone?"

"Here?" I glanced up at the mistletoe. "No," I said a little more sharply than I would have with someone else. Seth was… comfortable to be around. Easy to like. Probably easy to love. He'd already had his chance to hit my weak points and he'd passed.

But I didn't want to be in love.

Probably.

I narrowed by eyes at Seth.

He raised a hand in surrender. "Just asking. I know Patrick Miles is on site today. Half my staff are helping with Cozy's makeup just to get a glimpse. Maybe you were hoping—"

"Patrick is Ellen's crush," I said, cutting him off and turning away. "I'm counting mistletoe, not waiting under it."

"Sounds fun." Did the man's voice have to be so dangerously delicious?

Dang it. Seth was making me second-guess myself. I hated second-guessing myself. Like Mr. Darcy, I made my mind up about someone two-point-three seconds after I met them and moved on without so much as a backward glance.

But Seth was playing the clever Lizzie Bennet to my unflappable Darcy. The daisy-chained Persephone to my smiling Hades.

And, nope, picturing Seth with a pink flower crown resting in his sexily tousled platinum hair was not slowing down my train of thought.

"How many kisses would someone owe you if they walked toward you right now?"

Oh. Wow.

"Two hundred and seventy one," I said as I scrolled through the props list on my phone, desperately trying to think of something other than kissing Seth. *Oh, dang. Oh, frikkity-frak. Focus, Merri!*

I stole a quick glance and did not, absolutely did not, lick my lips.

Focus on the numbers, Merri.

"There are six mistletoe props on set right now, which means one is missing. I'll triple check, but I'm fairly certain the one that got away is the mistletoe bouquet from *A Stolen Christmas Kiss*."

How apropos.

Seth shook his head as his face wrinkled in confusion. "I don't know that one."

"The cat burglar breaks into the royal palace during the Christmas party, tries to steal the crown jewels and gets caught by the prince." I looked up, expecting some hint of recognition. "He catches her. They get a picture of them snapped. Everyone thinks they're dating. She tells him she wants revenge because her father made the crown jewels and they were stolen from him. Then, when they get married, all the crown jewels are made into a bouquet of mistletoe and holly?"

"Nope." Seth shrugged. "I guess I missed it."

"It came out the same year as *Scars*."

He shook his head again. "Sorry. I really don't watch a lot of Cozy romcoms. Or anything Cozy, actually."

I rolled my eyes. "You bought the company but never watched their major movies?"

"I pay people to do that."

"Right." Movie snob. Never mind that I only knew about the movie because Willow gave me a rundown of every famous Cozy prop and movie earlier, from the hand-painted gown in *Butterfly Kisses* to the authentic Viking sword replica from *A Viking's Heart*.

Cozy did historical romances. Who knew?

"Why are you counting props?" Seth asked. "This isn't an accountant's job. I know. I pay people to take care of the props."

I turned off my phone and walked to Seth at the end of Mistletoe Lane, very careful to look at his eyes, not his lips. "The numbers in the accounts are off. There's plenty of ways to hide money. Everything from fake lunches to overpaying workers. But I couldn't find another account and Cozy doesn't own a lot of land. Where most of their money goes is here."

Seth had gorgeous eyes, a warm, dark-chocolate brown.

Focus, Merri!

I waved a hand toward the contents of the warehouse. "Sets. Props. Costumes. Even with the money they save by getting brands to give them clothes, most of Cozy's hard-to-trace money winds up here. The cost of a one-of-a-kind prop is hard to quantify. It's easy to hide an overpayment."

"Right." Seth looked up at the mistletoe menace over our heads. "Wouldn't that take two? At least? If the buyer overpays, you still need a seller who will kick back some of the money, don't you?"

"Usually. It depends on how the seller was paid though."

I tapped his scythe to remind myself that I was not going to try any *Mistletoe Magic* of my own. The big, scary Slasher CEO did not want a girlfriend who looked like she was auditioning for the role of Glinda The Good Witch in *Wicked*.

Probably. "Did you come looking for me or were you headed somewhere with this?" I said, inclining my head at the scythe. There wasn't a good reason to run through a spring storm unless he needed to be here.

He spun it around. "Putting this back. I was checking on all the sets to see how people were doing, and this was laying around. Everyone's behind schedule since January was lost to negotiations. Rushed people get sloppy."

"I see." Not exactly the answer I'd been hoping for. A vivid imagination and a lackluster love life were not a good combination around Seth Morana. All practical considerations aside, I was more than willing to consider a fling with the Slasher CEO after I finished having a fling with his accounts. Two for one. Why not?

There so many reasons why not, but I had trouble remembering them every time Seth smiled at me.

"And..." His eyes narrowed as he walked to the rack of scythes adjacent to Mistletoe Lane.

"And?"

"There was a man who came looking for you. Bright green car, a bit of beard." Seth made a little grabbing gesture at his chin. "He was avoiding everyone from Cozy but asking everyone from Slasher if we'd seen you."

It wasn't a question but I could hear the hook all the same. Seth was *fishing*. Be still my heart. "Did he say why?"

Seth shook his head. "I told him I'd take him to find you if he signed the guest book. He made an excuse and ran for his car." The Slasher CEO fiddled with the scythes. "I don't usually get involved in anyone's private lives but... boyfriend? Ex? Co-worker? Father? Were you expecting someone? Should I have let him in?"

"Was he dressed like a twelfth-century Italian?"

"What would that—"

"Long, embroidered robes?"

"No."

"Then he's not my father." I ticked over all the other possibilities. "My office wasn't planning to send anyone over, and if they did they would have presented their credentials and signed in. I haven't had a second date in... years." I was not going to admit to how many.

"And the only stalker I'm aware of has four years before he's eligible for parole."

There was Harry from the Henderson account too, but I hadn't been back to the office to read his note. And it was hard to picture Harry coming to this side of town just to talk to me at work.

Seth's face made the journey from confusion to befuddlement to horror in record time. "Stalker?" Of course he got hung up on that, and not my father's commitment to historical recreation. "How do you say that so casually? That's a serious threat, not a missing sock. What if this guy is one? Should we call the police?"

I shrugged the worry away. "Probably another fan of my video. I get those still."

"What video?" Seth sounded genuinely confused.

Tucking my phone into my pocket, I looked up at him. His brow was furrowed, his whole face contoured with apparent confusion.

Award-worthy acting, but I wasn't buying it. "I was the star of a paste-a-face revenge porno after I told my high-school boyfriend I wasn't going to the same college as him. He made it and told me he'd delete it if I changed my mind."

Seth's eyes widened in horror and then his jaw set with anger. "That's illegal."

"Now, yes. At the time, I had trouble convincing the local judge, who'd known Wyatt since he was three, that I hadn't consented. My ex insisted I'd sent it to him. The video was up for seventeen months and it's still one of the first things that comes up when you search my name. I'm sure you've seen screencaps."

Everyone had.

Every college classmate.

Every brunch friend.

Every intern.

According to the video counter, everyone alive had seen a digital version of me getting indecent with the Christmas lights flickering at least twice.

"I didn't," Seth said, a rare flicker of anger crossing his face as he looked away. "I never watch those." He pulled his scythe closer like a security blanket. "When I made *Scars*, there were a lot of videos of me. Usually with people who thought they were fans. Sometimes with whoever I'd gone to dinner with that week. I watched one of myself." He looked away. "They say it's not as bad as actually being physically attacked, but…" He shrugged.

"I know." Sympathy was all I had to offer. "There's no way to erase it, is there? I can't forget it. Even when I try, there's someone reminding me."

Seth nodded. "Is that why you were worried this morning?"

"Yes." I took a deep breath and looked out at the rain cutting us off from the rest of the world. "I didn't enjoy our run-in at the pool this morning. I like controlling what people see."

Seth's eyes softened and I could feel my armor cracking a little more. "So, all this…" He gestured to my dress.

Smoothing a hand over my skirt, I widened my eyes and smiled like an innocent doll. "People see what they want to see. My ex wanted me scared of him, he wanted to use my body to punish me and control me. But I don't get scared. And I decided if I couldn't be anyone's dream girl, I'd become their nightmare woman: intelligent, beautiful, better than them in every single way. And I am." I ran a hand along my skirt and smiled. "I walk into a building looking feminine and frilly, and then I destroy people with a perfect smile on my soft, pink lips."

"Right." His expression grew guarded again as he put the scythe with the stack of others, neatly corralled by a pair of green bungee ropes. "The Grim Reaper of Chicago."

"You looked me up?" I guessed.

It was fair, I'd looked him up—double-checked to see if he was single, wondered for a few minutes about whether or not he had a type. A pointless waste of time, but fun.

Seth nodded thoughtfully. "The video didn't pop up in any of the internet searches."

"Ah, so you saw the Christmas firings." It wasn't a question.

"Basic business one-oh-one, isn't it? Know who you're dealing with." He shook his head. "I can't picture you firing that many people with a smile."

"I'm a grim reaper. I do everything with a smile." Three thousand, five hundred and one people lost their jobs on Christmas Eve because of me, and I had smiled for the cameras.

Seth tucked his hands into the pocket of his hoodie. "Was it easy for you?"

"Yes."

Seth's bio on the Slasher website had talked about his working-class roots. His mother had been a nurse, his dad did renovation; they'd lived just above the poverty line and both died before he graduated college. It was easy for him to see the mass layoff as a death sentence.

He stepped closer, eyes narrowing. "Do you know what happened to them after the firings?"

"Yes."

"How many of them died?" Another step.

"None."

"Really?" He was close enough to be threatening, or to kiss.

"Really." My smile grew wider. "In fact, several sent me notes in response to the New Year's Day cards I sent out. I believe in follow through and the personal touch."

His eyes narrowed. "You sent them all cards?"

"Yes. Mailed them out on Boxing Day."

Seth's scowl turned to an uncertain frown. He tilted his head in confusion.

"The day after Christmas."

His eyes narrowed. "What, you had Grinch remorse and spent Christmas looking for jobs for all of them?"

"Of course not. I did that the week of Thanksgiving."

Seth's smile started in his eyes, a twinkle of smug confidence that spread and turned his baleful glare to a radiant beam. He looked like he'd won a bet with himself. It was hard not to reach out, grab a fistful of his hoodie, and close the gap between us.

He didn't need to know the details, but since I was dropping secrets like beads at a Mardi Gras parade, I might as well throw this one in as a bonus.

"The company was going to transfer all their contracts unilaterally and start all the workers as new hires, with minimum pay. People who had spent nineteen years at the company would lose their retirement. Seniority was gone. I convinced the company to fire them instead. Severance pay was included, and they assumed all the employees would roll over and take the new contracts being offered. The union leaders and I met, and every single one of those people had a job offer before the new year. Most had at least four to choose from. All paying better than the job they'd lost. The company folded before February."

"I thought your job was to make the company better," Seth said.

"It is. And, in this case, the best thing for that company to do was shut down, because it was run by a greedy idiot embezzling from his own coffers." I knew my smile was cold and I didn't care. "The media was so outraged about the number of people fired that they never bothered to ask why."

No one ever asked women why. There was only judgment, never understanding.

"And so the world moves on, with my reputation as world's worst woman confirmed for the masses. The man in the green car might have been here for me, but don't worry, you're not liable if I get attacked on your premises. Sloan and Markham has a very good life insurance policy on me. So do my parents."

Seth blinked as he stepped away. "Right. Green car. That's what we were discussing."

"And missing mistletoe." I didn't like the sudden distance between us, but I didn't chase him either. If Seth didn't want to dance, that was his choice. My smile never wavered. "Maybe you should get back to work. The world is waiting for your horror movies with jump scares and spooky, whatever-flavor-of-monster it is that everyone wants this year. And I should be hunting down that little lost mistletoe bouquet that wandered away from home." Yup. That's exactly what I should have been doing.

Not waiting for Seth Morana.

Not hoping for anything.

He licked his lips as his gaze dipped to the ground and thunder rolled overhead. Rain hammered the rooftop.

I headed toward the large bay door. The cards were on the table, and like Kenny Rogers said, you needed to know when to walk away.

"Merri." Seth's voice caught me. "That's not why I do it. That's not why I make horror movies. I like fear, and I like being scared sometimes, but I don't think scared is sexy."

I hid a bitter smile as I stopped to watch the storm outside the doors. "I didn't say you did."

"What I like in horror stories is seeing someone scared, and then getting back up again. It may not have a happy ending, but they fight. They don't give up. Ever."

"You don't need to explain." He needed to stop talking so I could walk away, close the door. A part of me *liked* Seth Morana. He was smart enough to make connections, he didn't back down, he actually listened, which was a rare trait. I never needed anyone's approval. But I *wanted* his. And that terrified me.

"I know you don't need anything, but I want to explain. I'm like you. I do this because it's what feeds my soul. It's what I'm good at."

Seth's footsteps echoed between the snow-flecked pines and empty coffins of the warehouse. Pride kept me from moving. I was Merri Kriesmas. I might walk away, but I didn't run.

"The sexiest woman I've ever seen was the one who walked into my company and said she was going to steal my soul."

My cheeks warmed at the compliment, but I didn't turn around.

"You walked into my office and you stole the light. Everything else was dark, but somehow you made the room glow. A radiant moment of spring, full of color and joy, and when anyone else would have backed down or taken the easy out, you stayed. It would have been so easy for you to walk away, to make an excuse and leave Cozy with their cursed financials, but you didn't. I admire that."

I was a hundred percent not crying. The warehouse was dusty.

Seth stopped a little ways behind me, his shadow stretching out in front of us. "I'm not asking for anything. I just... thought you should know."

"Thank you." I managed to get the words out without sounding like I was falling apart. Over the years I'd been called many things—but somehow compliments were in short supply.

Being hated was easy. Being admired was… strange.

Rolling my shoulders back, I cleared my throat. "I'm just waiting for the rain to let up a little. Then I'll be on my way."

There was the soft sound of fabric moving and Seth's hand appeared in front of me holding a black umbrella.

"Thank you." I took it, all too aware of the heat of his body beside me. Looking would kill me.

There were good reasons not to flirt with Seth now.

Professional ethics.

Sort of.

This was a pro bono case and I was working for Ellen, so it was a gray area.

Okay, literally no one would care if I did flirt with him. Except maybe Seth. Who seemed open to the idea.

My mind was a dizzy twirl of Maybes and Whatifs.

I focused on the handle of the umbrella. It was ornate blackened wood, carved in the shape of a raven, with opal and mother-of-pearl inlays and dark red ruby accents. I'd seen the original prop certificate for it, and the price.

The price had included real opals.

I wiped a rogue tear away as I stared at the dazzling rainbow of fake opals. Slowly, I opened the umbrella, searching for what I already knew I'd find, mind spinning away down a path of lost dollars and false accounts.

Oretega.[20] The name was carved into the cane of the umbrella.

Too late, I realized Seth was still standing there as the silence stretched awkwardly between us. My grip on the umbrella tightened as I turned to him with a smile. I was done being dizzy. "Seth?"

He looked up at me, dark eyes filled with admiration and doubt.

I took a deep breath. "Will you marry me?"

"Marry you?" Seth stared at me, eyes wide with shock and—possibly—hope. "I—I'm not saying no. But divorce is expensive. And I… talk during movies?"

I stifled a giggle. "That's your worst trait? Talking during movies?"

His forehead wrinkled adorably as he tried to think. "Yeah, I think. That's probably the worst I do."

"I think I'll survive," I said stepping closer so I could tug at the pocket of his hoodie. "I just want to do all the things people do when they're madly in love and newly engaged."

---

[20] Oretega Mineral Exchange, not a single company, but a co-op of jewelers, vendors, metalworkers, artisans. It's the best place in northern Illinois for anything involving gemstones or previous metals. They handle over sixty percent of the state's mineral sales and get away with it because it is, technically, a co-op.

"I'm very willing to do that." He was being very careful not to reach for me. "But we don't need a wedding for that. Do we?"

"Mmm, but I want to steal your last name. I want to go out in public, and flirt, and go ring shopping." I waggled my eyebrows.

Seth narrowed his eyes.

He really was very smart. I appreciated that.

"Have you ever stepped out of a movie and missed a major plot twist? And when you come back you have no idea what's happening and the villain is suddenly kissing the love interest?" He tilted his head down as he smiled at me. "I feel like I missed a plot twist here. We went from mistletoe," he pointed to Mistletoe Lane, "to your ex, to the umbrella, and now you're proposing marriage?"

"You did tell me I was sexy," I reminded him.

He nodded slowly. "I'm glad you heard that. But the triggering event seems to be the umbrella, so I'm not sure if confessing my admiration actually has anything to do with what's going on in your head."

I closed the umbrella and lifted the handle to his eye level. "What do you see?"

"Carved wood, opal, mother of pearl, and heat-treated rubies or garnets. I can't tell."

"The umbrella from *Ghost Of A Christmas Kiss*, one of Cozy's few supernatural romance movies." I pulled up the prop inventory on my phone. "This is the umbrella used for close ups. It was accidentally used in a fight scene where several gems were knocked loose. Where do you think they took it for repairs?"

Seth raised an eyebrow. "Oretega does the best gem work in the city."

My smile brightened. I loved it when I didn't have to hand-feed my clients information. "Most of Cozy's dealings with them include the name of the contractor or LLC that did the work."

At any given moment, Seth looked about as terrifying as a tulip. But somehow, when the shadows shifted and he set his jaw, he looked much more intimidating. "Most? Not all?"

"Not all," I said with a sweet smile.

Seth looked at me and nodded. "And the umbrella?"

"The umbrella originally had real opals and three rubies, two with inclusions. These opals are fake, and the rubies are lab created. I'd bet my buttons on it."

"How can you tell?"

"Look." I pointed at the gems. "Synthetic opals are cheaper, and they have a much more regular color pattern. These look almost pixelated. The rubies? Flawless and dyed. There's no marks in them at all. Oretega had all the original gems handed in. One opal was listed as cracked, and a natural opal mined in Australia was bought to replace it." I tapped the handle. "None of these are natural. And a synthetic costs about a fifth of what the mined ones cost."

Another nod. "So where'd the money go?"

"That's what I'd like to find out."

"Am I coming along because I'm readily available, or can I feel special that you proposed to me?"

It was impossible to tell from his expression, but he sounded a little hurt by the idea. I guess not even the big, bad reaper man of Slasher Studios wanted to come in sec-ond place to Noah The Props Guy or whoever else might have wandered in here.

I tucked my phone back into my pocket and shook my head. "You are coming along because you are charming, charismatic, attracted to me, and even if you weren't all of those things, you're a fantastic actor who could fake it for a few hours. You will be the witty, debonair, wealthy man shopping for something sparkly for your fiancée—and maybe some cash back on the side where the insurance won't notice—and I'll play the ditzy—"

"Fiancée," Seth cut in before I could use something a little less complimentary.

"I look the part." I shrugged because he seemed upset at the implication. "Silly pink dress. Silly curled hair. Silly girl too stupid to know she's being used and going to be tossed aside as soon as someone better comes along."

"Do people actually treat you like that?"

"All the time." A wave of regret washed over me and I let it go with a rueful sigh. "You're too easy to talk to, did you know that?"

Seth nodded.

"Far too easy." I narrowed my eyes playfully.

He smiled and looked down at his feet before glancing up at me through long lashes. "I suppose I should go get changed into something a little fancier."

I shrugged. "I think you look hot in a hoodie, but suit yourself."

"It's easier to convince people you're ready to spend a lot of money when your clothes say you've already *spent* a lot of money." He smirked. "I'll meet you outside Slasher's main doors in, say, half an hour?"

"Sounds like a plan."

He winked at me and walked into the rain whistling.

Why? Why had I asked Seth Morana to marry me? I looked up at the passing clouds as the last of the storm dripped off the eaves of the Slasher building into the puddle in front of my feet. What colossal fit of madness had possessed me?

Ring shopping on a Saturday afternoon? I had minions for this. And, as I sat down on the wooden bench on the sidewalk outside Slasher headquarters, watching the drips falling from the eaves, I tapped my phone on my thigh and considered calling a minion.

I knew the answer to why, of course. I'd been the stand-alone *She* in my *Nanigans* for a long time. Using the office staff felt a little like cheating, and a lot like stealing someone's well-earned weekend.

Plus, this technically wasn't a Sloan and Markham operation.

But asking Seth to come with me?

That was my fault. Mostly.

If he'd followed the script and run away at the mention of marriage the way most people do, it wouldn't have been a problem. He could have brushed me off. He could have said no. He could have laughed in my face.

He had a plethora of options and he went with, *'I'm not saying no…'*

I rolled my eyes.

A bright orange sports car with a black racing stripe on the lateral line screeched to a halt in front of the building, sending a wave of water spraying over the sidewalk. It was, I had to admit, a theatrical opening and a beautiful shot.

The tinted window rolled down and Seth Morana grinned out at me. "Hiya, Killer."

"Hello, Lover." A smile hid all my worries. I stood up, brushing off my skirt and grabbing my tiny satin clutch that matched my blue shoes, my hair fascinator made of blue pearlescent beads, and the blue hydrangeas on my skirt.

Seth had changed into a matching blue shirt and black slacks that made my casual estimation of his net worth jump up by several tax brackets. "You like?"

"I like. We're the cute, matchy couple."

"It's mostly by accident," Seth said as I buckled in. "I didn't have time to run home, so I had to raid the offices for something that fit. Nicah let me borrow his car and his clubbing clothes."

"Those are clubbing clothes?"

"Gay bars have standards." Seth shrugged.

Nicah obviously went to better gay clubs than the ones Lucky dragged me to. "He has impeccable taste."

"And six years working as a costumer and tailor," Seth said. "The man is magic." The Slasher CEO's eyes slid over me again. "You changed something, what is it? You were all business when I saw you and now you look… sparklier.”

“A layer of shimmery lip gloss and some eyeliner.” As he stopped at a red light, I turned so he could see my face.

Seth nodded. “Nicely done.” He handed me a box. “A little addition to your costume today.”

“Thank you.” I hesitated for a moment, then shook it off and opened the box. A sparkling diamond necklace and matching earrings managed to shine even under the heavy clouds overhead. “This is—” Unnecessary. Overdone. Ugly.

“Worth almost three hundred thousand.”

Oh sweet mother of pearl. “Why?”

“The originals are. Those are exact replicas made out of cubic zirconia. I thought they might make good bait. Besides, no one is going to believe I’m going to put a ring on your pretty finger if I haven’t already handed you some dazzle.”

“This is an atrociously gaudy necklace.”

“I’m promise to take it off as soon as we get home.” He shot me a billion dollar grin and a wink that had me falling in love.

I laughed. “Stop flirting. Or I’ll tell Ellen you want to revive your acting career as the romantic lead in one of Cozy’s holiday films.”

“No flirting?” The car pulled into traffic. “So, as the director for this afternoon’s scene, what’s your vision? Because I thought a newly engaged, madly in love couple would definitely be flirting. What do you want to see?”

"Everything."

Seth hummed in delight.

"Starting with Oretega's account books, if possible. I'll see those Monday either way, but if I could get them today, it might help. For the most part, I want to get a feel for the area. Check out various vendors and see what they offer. See who sounds like they're willing to cut a deal with a rich man trying to rip off his insurance, and who throws us out. I want to see who upsells their product and who'll try to convince you cubic zirconia is the same thing as a vintage diamond."

"And... if I confess I don't know anything about gems except they're sparkly? Is our date over?"

I gave him an appraising look. The correct answer was yes. I should have him drop me off at the doors while I called Alexi, Sloan and Markham's gem guy. But I didn't want to.

Seth's smile grew nervous. "Your silence is very telling."

"Mmm, I think you can fake your way through. Just make sure I get a look at every gem."

"And you'll be taking notes."

I tapped my head. "I have a good memory. Not eidetic, but good enough to get us through a few hundred gems and out so I can make notes later. Even if all the gems are real we'll find out more by seeing who reacts to your proposal than anything else."

"Fair enough. I'm the rich young man with money to burn, in love with a gorgeous woman—"

"—and you're too stupid to remember that gold diggers can be pretty," I said. "That's the role."

He laughed. "I guess I should be grateful you want me for my bank account, not my body."

"Really I just want your for your brains."

"Miss Merri…" He gave me a look that made me want to say yes to anything. "I thought you were trying to steal my time, not my heart."

"Well…" Yes. Right. We were acting. Of course. "Maybe there's room for some flirting today."

"And touching?"

"Keep it appropriate for a family-friendly production."

A speculative eyebrow went up. "We have to make the family first, so…"

"Seth Morana!" I could feel my cheeks turning red as a cherry.

"I… What? I was thinking an address and a dog. Where was your mind?"

I pressed my lips together and stared straight ahead. "Merri?"

I shook my head.

He laughed.

When I peeked over at him, he was blushing. "As long as you don't suggest shopping for tables," I said, "we'll probably get through this okay."

"Tables?" He stopped at a red light and studied me. "Why did tables come up in this conversation?"

"No reason." I shook my head and refused to make eye contact. "Definitely not a concern for today."

"So we'll *table* that conversation for later?"

We both were giggling as the Oretega building loomed on the horizon.

Oh. This was so, so very bad. I had to run an investigation, play the dizzy girlfriend, and cuddle up to Seth Morana for the rest of the afternoon, and I had to do it all while not falling in love with a charming, intelligent, sexy man who was doing his best to win me over.

Heaven help me.

I was supposed to be saving Cozy, not getting caught by the Curse.

The Oretega Mineral Exchange was on the edge of Bridgeport off of South Ashland and Pershing. It was an old brick building with towers and art deco arches. The north end was three stories of red brick and wide, industrial windows with the solar panel glazing that had been so popular two decades ago. The watchtower was six stories, soaring over the neighboring warehouses and originally meant to vent air back when the building had been a winery.

The building had housed many companies over the centuries. I wasn't sure what the grand total was, but now it was the Oretega Mineral Exchange, the one-stop shop for all of Chicago's mineral needs, from gravel to gold.

Seth parked in the lot along 38th Street and opened the car door for me. "Ready for your close up?"

I took his hand and stepped out of the car like I was about to walk the red carpet. "What do you think?"

"You're already a scene stealer."

It was hopeless, he had me giggling again. "You're so cheesy."

"You like it." He was smiling at me. Focusing on me.

And I did like it.

It had been so long since I'd been the center of attention—or at least the center of *positive* attention. I'd forgotten what it was like to have someone smiling at me because they were happy to see me.

No, not forgotten. Ignored.

All the years of coming in last place for everything, of being overlooked, of being hated… it had helped me build my armor. It had made me strong. And it had made me bury a part of myself away.

Being around Seth brought out a craving, a ceaseless hunger for attention and affection.

Heaven help me, but I wanted this. I *wanted* to be more important than my parent's history books, my sister's sports, my teacher's demands, my boyfriend's hobbies.

I wanted to be loved and adored and cherished.

I wanted Seth to keep looking at me like I was the only thing that mattered.

That's why I walked away, a pretty smile on my lips, as I shook my head.

I couldn't have Seth.

I couldn't be the center of his world.

I couldn't risk the heartbreak.

So I walked ahead of him, pulling my armor back on, composing myself until the fragile little girl I'd been, so desperate for any approval at all, was carefully locked behind layers of ferocious confidence and independence.

"Merri, stop."

I froze a few steps ahead of Seth. "What?"

"Twirl and look at the building?"

"Why?"

"The lighting is perfect."

I stepped, shifting my weight and letting my skirt and curls flare around me.

"Perfect." Seth was going to put Patrick Miles out of business with his smile.

"We stopped for perfect lighting?" I narrowed my eyes. "Who decorated the Slasher offices?"

I had a guess.

"Me and Alisson." Seth typed something into his phone and looked up at me. "Why?"

"Just a hunch." Now confirmed. I was on a date with an artist who had stopped to snap my photo because the lighting was good. He was so adorable doing it, I couldn't even be annoyed.

He held up his phone for my inspection.

Seth had been wrong: the lighting wasn't good, the lighting was fantastic. A slice of afternoon sunshine cut through the clouds to splash rainbows on the sidewalk's puddles and make my hair glow. He'd caught me mid-turn, looking sun-kissed and dewy without showing my face.

Underneath my photo was the caption, RED HOT IS MY FAVORITE FLAVOR.

"Red hot?"

"Cinnamon? Krisemas? Red curls? It works." Seth was watching my reaction.

"Are you really going to post that on your social feed?"

"If you approve it. I know you don't like pictures, so I won't if you don't want me to," Seth said. "Want me to tag you? I don't need to."

My eyes widened in amusement as I shook my head. "I don't have socials. So…"

So what?

The words *I don't care* died unsaid.

I did care. For years I'd kept layers of work and silence between me and the world, and now Seth was asking if I was willing to risk everything. Again.

Looking at the picture, I tried to see it as a stranger might, the artistic movement and the perfect lighting and the hint of romance. "I doubt anyone at Oretega is going to do a deep dive into your digital life to see if you're on a fake date."

"It's only fake because I'm not taking you out to dinner later," Seth said. His expression clouded. "Do you want me to delete it? It was just an impulse shot. Good lighting. Compelling composition. Great subject." His eyes lingered on me with a shy smile.

What was I more scared of?

Another paste-a-face porno? My face wasn't even showing.

The suggestion that Seth and I were more than passing acquaintances? …I could live with that.

Lifting my chin, I smiled. "Post it. Just know I'm not responsible for your heartbroken fans."

"They'll be fine," Seth promised as he posted the picture. "It's been at least a minute since I was in a real relationship. They'll enjoy the speculation."

In the time it took Seth to hit send and show me the screen, the image had garnered forty-seven responses including a wide-eyed *WOW!* from Alisson.

The phone chimed.

"Updates or death," Seth read aloud. He chuckled. "Maybe I should have told Alisson about our outing before we outed."

"Will you be in trouble?" I tried to peek at his screen to see what Alisson had really said.

Seth pulled the phone closer, reeling me in. "Can I take more pictures?"

"Will they all look as good as that one?"

"It would be impossible to take a bad photo of you."

"That's not true." Lucky had hundreds from our high school days.

"It is for me." The cocky grin that made Seth millions in minutes appeared.

I laughed as I rolled my eyes. "You are so sure of yourself!"

"Only because I know I'm that good!"

"Oh!" I shook my head as Seth reached for me. "Don't leave openings like that. I'll take them."

Sunlight blinded me for a moment as someone opened the door to Oretega and stepped out.

With my tiny blue clutch, I batted at Seth's arm playfully. "We're supposed to be looking at rings." My voice was pitched to carry, cheerful and bright.

His answering smile was equally dazzling. "I can't wait to see you in nothing but diamonds!"

"Seth!"

His hand was cold as it slipped down my forearm to touch my hands and lift my fingers to his lips for a kiss. With a little tug, he pulled me in so my arm was around his waist and our lips were a breath apart.

"Get out of my way!" A surly, male voice cut through the scene as a heavy hand pushed us toward the street. It wasn't a narrow sidewalk. The vaguely familiar man was large, but there was more than enough space for him to pass us without comment.

Seth glared after him.

"I guess they wouldn't take his coupon."

That did it. Seth broke into a laugh, holding me like there was a film crew circling us and an enraged hairdresser threatening his life if he ruined my curls. "You are just..."

"A lightning rod for angry men?" I suggested.

"A magnet?" Seth took my hand and we walked toward the door. "Magnet is better. There are fewer puns with lightning rod."

"Are you playing script doctor on our conversation?" I laughed.

A guilty expression crossed his face before his smile returned. "The downside of dating me. I like taking photos and I can't stop thinking about scripts."

"On the upside, you have killer good looks, a charming personality, and—ah—"

Seth opened the door for me and we stepped into a heavily air-conditioned lobby with a wooden block that came up to my chest and was probably meant to be a front desk, beige walls wrapped on the lower two-thirds by raffia, and faded, peeling brown linoleum on the floors.

My 'ah' turned an 'ugh.'

"Doesn't exactly inspire big spending," Seth said. "Maybe this is the gravel buyer's entrance."

"Maybe."

We wound our way through narrow side halls lined with old, waxed-cardboard file boxes that I suspected were for me on Monday.

"Problems?" Seth asked as his hand hovered just above my lower back, not quite touching, as we followed the sound of quiet chatter to the end of the warehouse with more light.

"Paper files are what people throw at me when they're hiding things. It means they weren't fully digital when the new law went into effect and they probably fudged more than a few numbers."

Another beige entryway, this time with a fake aspen tree in need of dusting, and then we walked into an area with white tile floors, crystal chandeliers, and artfully arranged coves of stones and gems. There were workshops with benches and soldering tools lined behind wooden, stone, and glass display cases. One very shimmery shop had a silver-and-glass display.

In attempt to overpower the scent of burning metal, someone had doused the area with a vanilla air freshener that reminded me of my middle school teacher's hand lotion.

"Camera," Seth whispered. "Lights."

I gave his hand a little squeeze. "Action."

"What do you think, sugarplum?" Seth asked in a voice pitched to carry.

I squealed like a six-year-old who'd been given free run of the cotton candy machine at the school carnival. "It's all so beautiful!"

"Not as beautiful as you." Seth made me believe it. The look in his eyes, the tilt of his body, the caress of his hand... For a moment he made me believe that there was nothing more important to him in the world than me.

"You're so perfect," I said for our ears only. It took effort to turn away from Seth's loving smile to look for our first victim. "Who looks extra scammy?"

"Eh, kind of a toss up between most the back row on the right and those four on the left."

"Good eye."

Finding quality in any city was about knowing the nature of the city. Chicago wasn't interested in glitz and glamour, but understated elegance and quiet superiority.

Classic. Timeless. Untouchable. Unknowable.

The shops Seth had picked up were going for dazzle. They were props for a photoshoot. The high prices covered the experience, not the materials.

"Let's try Three Promises," Seth said, pointing to a shop shaped to look like a wooded glen, complete with fake ancient oak and elegant Celtic knots.

"Sounds... promising?" I waited to see if Seth approved of the word play.

"Cute." He smiled and led the way to the shop with an expansive stride. Seth took up space, filled the room and made people watch.

I watched him for a moment, took a deep breath of the vanilla-scented air, and went after him. It was just a job. No different than walking into any office in my brightly colored dresses and being mistaken for someone's girlfriend or intern.

Under the fake, moss-covered oak with green silk leaves that filtered the bright overhead lights, the Three Promises shop had metalwork elegantly displayed on small plinths.

Seth seemed more interested in the lighting setup that put each display stand in a spotlight rather than the rings and necklaces on display.

The sole occupant was an older man with a head of thick, white hair, a matching goatee that came to a point, bright blue eyes, a mustard-yellow shirt, and a warm smile. "Good afternoon, folks. Are you out for a stroll or looking for something particular?"

"Oh, I found someone I want to keep," Seth said giving me a hungry look that could be threatening or seductive depending on the lighting. "Now I'd like to find something enchanting to keep her by my side."

I rolled my eyes where the silversmith couldn't see. The cheese levels were high enough to drown the nachos.

"Necklace?" the silversmith asked. "Rings? Earrings? Bracelets? How do you feel about bracelets?"

"Rings. Something sparkly for me," I said. "Something classic for him."

"Sparkly?" The man nodded. "All right, all right. Let's see what I have. Tanzanite, morganite, moissanite is very popular at the moment. Clear like a diamond, nearly as hard, but I can give you the name and number of the family who mined it. There is no blood on my gems. No conflict." He waved a hand in the air, dismissing the very idea. "Here, here, have a look."

He set a small, cherrywood box on the display counter. The lid was carved with pictures of winged fairies dancing in the moonlight; it lifted to show a line of beautiful rings. Soft purples, radiant blues, pale yellows, and delicate greens mixed with gems so pure they caught the showroom lights and sparkled like captured stars. The metal of the rings had been twisted into fanciful vines and waves.

Seth stepped beside me and then hesitated, hand hovering over my waist as if unsure of his reception.

I snuggled closer as I ooed and ahhed appreciatively over the rings. They were all very... ring-like. I had no frame of reference. My jewelry interests had never extended past hair fascinators and those unfortunately bedazzled jeans in middle school that we will never talk about again.[21]

---

[21] My mom was going through what she called a Modern Vintage stage where she wanted to show us all the life skills people had used during the plague years of the early 21st century to create art at home, but she hated embroidery and knitting, so she spent an afternoon gluing rhinestones to my pants before she gave up in boredom and went back to churning butter.

"What do you think?" Seth asked. "Should I get you one to match every dress you have?"

"Am I getting a wedding ring for every color of the rainbow?"

The silversmith chuckled. "Not sure anyone wants to go to a red wedding."

Seth and I watched him politely, hoping he'd get to the punchline of his joke.

"No?" The man shook his head. "Well, I got that reference." He sighed and snickered to himself over something I missed entirely.

"Try one on," Seth urged, nudging the ring box toward me.

After a moment's indecision, I picked a delicate rose gold ring with an intricate leaf pattern holding a pale-pink morganite gem cut to look like a rose about to bloom. The carving should have ruined the faceting of the gem and left it without the luminous shine that traditionally cut gems had.

It didn't. The little rose glowed like magic.

"Hold it up." Seth had his phone out again.

A quick shot, and I moved to the next ring. They looked and felt real to me. None of the gems had the brittle-bright clarity of lab-created stones or the marks of inferior gems being passed off at a higher price.

After a thorough inventory of the rings, I dazzled the silversmith with a smile. "Can we see the wedding bands, please?" I eyed Seth like meat at the market. "Let's start with silver..."

"You like me in silver?" Seth raised an eyebrow.

"I like you in anything," I said, then leaned closer. "And out of everything," I whispered just loud enough to make the silversmith blush.

Seth turned so our heads were close together, lips almost touching. "Flirt."

"Tell me you don't like it."

The tenderness and appreciation in his eyes was almost my undoing. Seth Morana was either the best actor in the history of theater, or he was half in love with me.

"I like everything you do."

The silversmith's polite cough kept me from following through on the invitation in Seth's eyes. "Perhaps one of these rings?"

"Mmm, yes." I tore my attention away from Seth to the display of wedding bands. Hammered silver and gold, vined and twined metals. Bold Celtic knots and other intricate weavings that all looked authentically expensive.

While Seth made a show of trying them on, I perused the rest of Three Promise's display case and flipped through their digital look-book of custom art.

I'd verify it all on Monday, but I had a hunch that Three Promises was one of Oretega's big earners, and that everything sold here in the fairytale glen was precisely what they said it was.

"Merri," Seth's voice caught my attention, "what do you think?"

The silver ring he was wearing had a scroll pattern with a dark obsidian inlay.

"Interesting. It doesn't look Celtic."

"It's Slavic," Seth said. "My grandfather had one like it."

"Your family is Slavic?"

"I thought the name was a giveaway." Seth twisted the ring off and handed it back to the silversmith.

"Seth isn't Slavic."

"Morana is." He grinned at me.

Dangit, now I was going to have to look his name up and figure out what amused him so much.[22]

Seth touched my arm and leaned in for what probably looked like a kiss on my cheek. "I have a line on some less reputable players. Wanna go hunting?"

"I'll be right there," I said with a demure smile. I waited for him to meander away before turning back to the silversmith. "Give me the price for the ring and your business card, please."

"You like it?" Bushy eyebrows went up in surprise.

"I'm ambivalent about it, but he likes it."

"It might be out of your price range…"

A part of me wanted to buy up the whole store just to prove him wrong. I'm a Kriesmas. I come with a competitive streak pre-installed at birth. But I managed to turn my savage need to win into a cutting smile. "Let me worry about that."

"Of course." The man scribbled a large number on the back of the card.

------

[22] I looked it up. Morana means death in Slavic. Ha ha. The CEO of Slasher Studios is named Seth Death. His sense of humor slays me some times.

"And his ring size." I was playing for keeps.

The silversmith handed me the card. "I'm here Tuesdays through Saturdays, no holidays. And I have two weeks off in July."

"Understood." I flipped his card over. "Glen O'Connell."

Glen nodded.

"Have a good day." Smiling, I tucked the card into my purse. Before I could think about happily ever after, I had to find Cozy's missing cash.

I waved goodbye to Glen and followed as Seth began schmoozing the other shop owners. A little off-color joke there. A little hint of tax avoidance there. A little song and dance to convince everyone he was One Of Those Guys.

How they missed the sharpness in his dark eyes, I'm not sure. Seth looked angry.

Much more angry than I needed him to be. I strutted over like the floors of Oretega Mineral Exchange were the catwalks of Milan and caressed Seth's arm, drawing all his attention to me.

One glance and the anger in his eyes blew away like ash. "Hello, beautiful."

"Hello." I practically purred the word as I leaned just so, giving everyone the hint of a peek of a look at what was hiding under my bodice. The suggestion of the forbidden was enough to disrupt whatever conversation was happening. "Find anything you like?"

"I found you," Seth said, lifting my hand to his lips for a cold kiss.

"Is that what happened? I thought I'd found you."

Green light sparkled in the edge of my vision. I turned to look at a display case of lab-grown gems carved into a variety of shapes: frogs, cars, buildings. All in bright, emerald green.

A tall, thin man with pale skin and mousy brown hair dangled himself over the counter like a lost rag doll. "You like the carvings?"

"Are they yours?" I asked.

The man shook his head. "They're Reggie's." He tapped the name of the shop owner on a tiny display plaque.

Reginald Yerke.

Yerke.

I'd run across that name before. It appeared frequently in the Cozy books, there was a Yerke LLC in the Windy City Security's books, and it had come up two years ago in a conversation about an expert witness in a trial I'd also been a witness for.

Interesting.

On Monday I'd have the interns run a check to see if they were connected in any way. Yerke wasn't the most common of names, but Chicago was a large city.

Seth fiddled with his camera, playing at examining lighting and angles. "Want to try something on?"

"All of it." I smiled at the ragdoll of a man. "Can you let me see that ring?" I pointed to one with a chunky gold band and a bright blue sapphire.

"Um, Reg can, as soon as he comes in." The man looked over his shoulder. "He stepped out just a minute ago to talk to someone. Ah!" The man stood straighter. "Here he is! Reg!"

The burly man from the pool this morning, now with a lime green track suit and a bag from Heavenly Monday's. That at least explained why he'd seemed familiar outside—and his rush to run us off the sidewalk: there was a midday sale on macarons.

"Reg," the lean man said, "meet... ah..."

"Seth and Meredith," Seth said. "Soon to be Mister and Missus."

"Congratulations!" the younger man beamed.

Reg burped. "You want wedding rings?"

"I want everything!" My megawatt smile hit a vantablack shield around Reg Yerke.

His lip curled up in a sneer.

"I want her to have everything," Seth said, slipping an arm around my waist and pulling me back for a hug. "And I have the money to give her what she wants."

Yerke's eyes lit up with greed. "In that case, let me show you our premier collection."

Premier... Right.

Seth pulled me closer than he had all day, lips brushing my ear. "Does he look familiar?" The words were almost inaudible.

I nodded slightly, fully aware that the lean man and several of Reggie's friends were watching our very public display of *affection*.

"He's the one who came looking for you earlier." Seth kissed my head as he stepped away.

Yerke had come looking for me? At Slasher studios? I tried adding that fact to my equations, searching for a connection.

If he knew I was coming to Oretega on Monday, why

look for me at Slasher? Why come to me early and off-site at all? Unless he wanted to tell me something he didn't feel safe saying here.

I looked at the row of eager jewelers in the their dazzling shops. On Monday, I'd have full files on all of them. For now I had a row of suspects.

"Here," Yerke said, offering me a hand to lead me to a little chair. He took my clutch and set it to the side as he pushed a box of shiny rings in front of me. They were quite pretty, in a generic sort of way. Emeralds and diamonds on simple gold and silver bands. A few sapphires. Two rubies. "What do you want to try on first?"

"That one!" I pointed to the largest clear gem, with water-fine clarity like cut glass.

"Excellent choice." Yerke's voice dripped with snake oil. "You have an eye for gems."

If I did, I wouldn't be shopping here. The ring was too light to be real gold and the stone too clear to be diamond, white sapphire, or moissanite. Still, I held it up and posed as Seth took pictures.

Ring after ring.

Necklace after necklace.

We worked our way down the row of jewelers with me modeling the fake gems and Seth photographing everything as he charmed and winked and lied to everyone. Before the hour was over, my brain felt bloated with information. I needed to sort all of this, collect Seth's reports on who had offered him what cutbacks, and check it against the list of props.

"You okay?" Seth asked as I listed sideways. "You're looking a little pale."

"Just a little hungry." A tiny white lie. Food could wait, but I couldn't stuff another fact into my head right now.

"Let's go get something to eat and figure out what you liked best," Seth said, staying in character. He slipped the last ring off my hand and returned it to the jeweler. "What are you hungry for?"

I smiled up at him. "Whatever you like best."

"Ah, here." Yerke held out the clutch I'd left at his shop as I was whisked down the row. "And my card." He added it to the top. "Please do come back." He winked at Seth.

"I will," Seth promised with an easy smile.

As we walked away, I turned the business card over twice, looking for clues. If Yerke was going to slip me information, this would have been the best way to do it.

"I lost you somewhere, didn't I?" Seth asked as he held open the door. "Was the hug too much?"

"Hmm?" I tried to pull my attention back to him, but Seth didn't fit into the equation here. "Sorry? My mind wandered."

"Yeah." His smile was sad as he opened the door for me.

I buckled myself in and waited for Seth to put his phone in the slit between our seats. "Can I look at the photos?"

"Be my guest." He unlocked the phone for me.

One by one I reviewed the pictures. "This is good. Can I send it to my phone?"

Seth nodded. "Sure."

"Why do you have a photo of Yerke's business card? There was nothing there worth buying."

"He offered me a deal." Seth's lips lifted in a smug smile.

"Oh? What'd he offer?"

"Morgan slid me the name of an appraiser who will certify cubic zirconia as real diamonds for the insurance company."

And there it was. The first unraveling thread, waiting to be pulled.

If workspace decor was a reflection of personality or mental health, Ellen needed to schedule an appointment with a therapist. The office space was grungy, with sickly yellow paint peeling off the walls, revealing patches of mint green and industrial beige. Odd streaks of black from old tape filled the gaps between notices, pictures, budgets, and memos that were pinned in every reachable amount of wall space.

I eyed the sagging ceiling of the office as I took a seat gingerly in a black rolling chair that squeaked in fright and smelled like it had been rescued from the dump.

Ellen sat behind a wobbly old desk that might have been green in a previous life, but was now so scratched and dented that all that could reliably be said about it was that it was a metal of some form, and that Ellen took her dedication to recycling a little too far. That thing should have been melted for scrap before we were born.

"So…" Ellen pulled out a small, pink box and lifted the lid to hit me with the strategically aimed scent of lemon and chocolate. She'd brought cupcakes from my favorite shop. "How did your date with tall, dark, and dangerous go?"

Two cupcakes nestled in the bakery box like little jewels. One with a cheerful pink raspberry swirl of frosting on the tempting body of a lusciously delicious chocolate cake. One a pale golden lemon frosting on a yellow lemon drop cupcake with the Midwest's best lemon curd inside.[23]

Ellen tipped her head to the side with a smile as she relaxed back into her chair, the beautiful pieces of temptation resting on her lap. "What do you think?"

"I think you have either a line to my assistant, or a very good memory," I said, nodding at the cupcakes. Would Willow give out privileged information about my favorite cupcakes?

…Maybe?

"Remember when we first had these?" Ellen asked.

"Eighth grade field trip to the museum. You and I snuck away from our group because Marial's mom was on the phone and Marial wanted to be with her boyfriend. We used your phone and walked two blocks to buy cupcakes and made it back before anyone noticed."

"I bet you remember Marial's boyfriend's name too."

"Hunter," I said. "He was in Mister Feldman's class. Played basketball in high school. Tore his ACL junior year. Came out as bi his first year in college. Graduated

---

[23] That's not my opinion, it's Zagat's.

in three years with a degree in sports medicine. Worked for the Olympic gymnastics team. Married a coach from the woman's team." I blinked. "Did you need to know that? Why are you quizzing me?"

Ellen held the box out. "Pick one."

I grabbed the lemon cupcake with immodest haste and far less grace than Ellen showed plucking up the chocolate and raspberry confection.

"So the date went poorly?"

The cupcake was almost in my mouth. "What date?"

"With Seth Morana!" Ellen laughed, nibbling daintily on her cupcake like she couldn't inhale it in one bite.[24]

She pulled out her phone and turned it so I could see the screen.

RED HOT IS MY FAVORITE FLAVOR.

…Seth was right, the lighting was perfect. The sunbeams caught the red fire of my hair, made my pink A-line dress with its bright blue hydrangeas stand out in sharp relief against the shadows of the rain-washed street.

Ellen bit into her cupcake with smug satisfaction. "I am, last I checked, your best friend in the entire world, and I expect an update."

"It's fake." I turned the screen off and pushed the phone back toward Ellen. The cupcake didn't sound so appealing any more. "I thought it would make more

---

[24] No, seriously. You should have seen her eat after wrestling practice. Ellen is tiny but mighty, and she has the appetite to match.

sense if we went ring shopping as a couple. It looked more natural than me stomping in and grilling people."

"But you stomp so well." Ellen rested her elbow on the wobbling desk and continued nibbling at her cupcake. "And you let him take a picture."

"Not of my face. No one will recognize it."

"Because everyone in Chicago dresses like you? In custom, hand-sewn dresses? Really? I mean, I didn't even to need to know it was Morana's account to recognize you."

Yup. I was done eating. "You're my best friend."

"Merri, I love you to pieces, but you can either tell me, or I can call my mom and tell her where to look."

My eyes went wide at the threat. "You would not."

The Midwest grapevine would end with my family and then I would never hear the end of it. If my mother knew I'd been on a date she'd be picking out wedding invites by Wednesday.

Ellen turned her phone back on with a flick of her thumb and slowly scrolled through Seth's social media feed.

The aesthetic before today was the Slasher brand: black, white, gray… An assortment of hoodies and neon goths and mint tea in his Final Boss mug. Every single shot was done with the precision and care of someone who not only understood light and shadow, but who loved playing with them. Seth was an artist with an artist's soul and love for his medium.

And then there was the shot of me in the sunlight, turning away. The classic Slasher colors but with something more added. A warmth that added something like ginger giving a cake an extra pop you never knew was missing.

More photos followed. Rings. The necklaces. Pieces of me falling in between the shots of Seth's life as if I'd always been there. The captions were all complimentary with a teasing, flirtatious tone that came across as sincere affection.

"So Seth writes good ad copy. He knows how to work a camera. We knew this already."

"Did he ask?" Ellen's jaw was tight. She didn't like confrontation, but if I told her that Seth had taken those photos without consent, she'd march up to his office and all the police would find later would be a suspicious hint of bleach in the air and a missing tarp from the props warehouse.

I put on my prettiest smile. "He did. And I said yes, because it's all work related."

"Hmmm." Ellen put her phone away.

"You don't need to worry about me. I'm fine."

"Liar." She finished her cupcake while I stared at mine. "You like citrus flavors when you're stressed, chocolate when you're calm. You went out with Seth, had more photos of you taken than anyone has taken since our eighth grade dance when Jordy had a camera and too many pixie sticks, and you're eating lemon cupcakes."

I folded my hands in my lap, smile undimmed. "It is so much easier to lie to everyone else."

"Is that why you didn't talk to me after high school?"

The streaks of dirty wall blurred a little.

It wasn't tears. It was allergies. The office was very, very dusty. "I'm sorry I didn't keep in touch. It was a hard year."

"It's my fault." Ellen reached out and squeezed my arm above the elbow. "I was busy and I kept telling myself you'd reach out if you needed anyone."

"I would have. If I needed help, I would have asked." There would need to be a shattering reversal in the laws of the universe before I admitted I needed help, but I would ask if I needed it.

Delegating was different. Research minions and the interns who checked my email weren't helping to help, they were well paid to share my workload.

A tiny, treasonous part of me pointed out that I'd asked Seth for help, but I assured myself that was completely different. I didn't *ask* for *help*. I'd invited him to come along to Oretega as a favor to him. His company was involved.

"It's just that I know how you think," Ellen said quietly. "I know you don't like cameras. And Morana isn't easy to get along with."

"He was an ideal shopping companion," I said reaching for the lemon cupcake because I was not going to let it go to waste on the twisted pain of my memories. "He knows how to talk to people. He's charming."

Ellen raised both eyebrows. "Morana? Seth Morana? The Dark Lord of Slasher in his oversized hoodie and silent stares? He's charming?"

"When he wants to be."

Ellen looked at her phone again with a thoughtful frown.

"What?"

"Nothing, just a thought. You always did notice personality first, didn't you?"

"I mean, I appreciate a hot body as much as the next person—maybe more since I think both guys and girls are hot?—but yes, personality is what I care to notice. I notice how people react to me. I do notice aesthetics and beauty too, but if there isn't a mind to match..." I shrugged. Liking smart people who could keep up in a conversation was not relevant to the case. "Do you want to hear what we found?"

Ellen dropped the phone in favor of gossip. "I hope it was a big pile of cash marked 'Cozy Film Budget'."

"Not quite, but there are appraisals that were definitely oversold. Props bought, appraised, and sold at a higher value."

She frowned. "How does that make Cozy less money? The props were in the budget."

"Rapid money flow and extra props and repairs." I ticked the losses off on my hand. "Someone at Cozy overpaid. In some cases they double-paid, marking it as a replacement piece. The money went to Oretega."

"Someone at Cozy wasn't good with accounts."

"No, someone at Cozy had a deal on the side. The computers you had were all bought as part of the company, the software included. For you and Seth to both log in and see separate accounts, someone in the office had to do that."

Ellen leaned on her desk. "My computer is new, though."

I raised an eyebrow. "Since when?"

"The one I was working on got dropped when we were shuffling around offices. It was a mess, so I brought in my laptop."

"Is that when you noticed the discrepancy?"

She nodded slowly.

"Then someone programmed the computers to give you false amounts." It would be so easy for someone with the right skills to create an extra admin account. A secret back door that scheduled withdrawals and hid them. It'd happened before, and I'd even suspected it in Dulcie's case, but our tech people hadn't been able to prove it. I made a mental note to get someone from the office to check out who'd programmed Cozy's digital security.

"What would have happened?"

"Eventually you would have overdrawn and gotten a notice from the bank." I dropped my empty cupcake wrapper in the recycling bin by Ellen's desk. "Which doesn't make sense. That would get someone caught. Fast."

"If they already had the money, why go through all this?" Ellen asked.

I tried several scenarios in my mind. The company had changed hands in January. The discrepancy hadn't appeared until April. Dates and numbers waltzed through my head. "Oh, that's almost clever."

"What is?"

"They hid the money from the sale in the Cozy accounts, but left a back door to empty the accounts. Taxes are due next week. I bet they planned on taking the money after. If they could frame someone still working here, so much the better."

"But, then, the money should be here. All the money they embezzled through the props should still be here."

"When did the bank account glitch?"

"My computer broke Monday. I noticed the accounting error Thursday afternoon, right before I called your office."

"Something spooked them." Someone had pulled the plug early.

No, that still couldn't be right. It didn't make sense. All the original conspirators were gone. The original money was gone.

I shook my head.

Something was missing from my equation and I didn't know what.

Ellen sighed. "I'm sorry I dragged you into this. It's a mess, and I can't even pay you to solve the problem properly."

"It's all right. What are best friends for if not rushing into wild and dangerous situations together?"

"Exactly." Her smile was brilliant and terrifying. Last time she'd looked like that I'd been volunteered for the high school math team.

"I just walked into a trap, didn't I?"

Ellen's smile widened. "Just a teeny-tiny one."

"I should have known. Those were cupcakes of bribery, weren't they?"

"There's an art charity thing tonight." Ellen's hand fluttered. "A big thing at the museum downtown. Food. Silent auction. Live music. We're all supposed to go and

I have the actors all showing up together, but I need a Plus One."

"Me?"

"Pllleeeaaase?" Ellen begged. "I will owe you cupcakes for the rest of my life. Or meals. Or tickets to premier night. Anything. Absolutely anything, just please don't make me go alone. All of the important people from Slasher are going, and me. I'm already..." She waved at herself as if to say she wasn't impressive enough. Credit where it was due, Ellen knew how to push my buttons. The very thought that someone would dismiss her was reason enough to go. "I'm in. When is it?"

"We need to be there in sixty minutes."

I closed my eyes and silently cursed in Latin, Greek, English, Middle English, Scots, and then listed my top ten favorite Shakespearean insults. "Sixty minutes? I hope daywear is appropriate, because I can't get home and change fast enough."

"I actually have some options. Kurt in costuming said Slasher had some dresses we could look at." She bit her lip and gave me an apologetic smile.

It was a good thing I didn't believe in reincarnation, because if I did, I could only accept I had done something truly horrendous in a past life, like coughing on people during flu season.[25]

---

[25] Okay, maybe I'm exaggerating. Going to a charity gala in Chicago is way better than what those people would come back as if they reincarnated. I bet they would come back as maggots.

Ellen dragged me down the empty halls of the quiet studio to a terribly small dressing room with shiny, eggshell-blue walls that smelled of fresh paint and cologne. The wide, dark blue couch looked comfortable enough to nap in.

For a second, I let it tempt me.

But Ellen had dresses for us to try on and we had hair to do before our cab arrived.

For Ellen I picked a shimmering amethyst gown with elegant pleats and just enough color gradient to give her extra height. It was elegant and modern without being gaudy enough to draw criticism.

With her hair drawn back by a matching gold-and-amethyst tiara, she looked like the queen of the gods ready to rule the world.

While Ellen did her makeup, I sorted through the remainder of the dresses. A bright red one was out. So was the short gold one. The silver one was too narrow in the shoulders.

Finally I picked up a black-and-white abomination that Ellen and I had been carefully avoiding. The under-layer started black at the top and fell from one shoulder into silver and then to a radiant white. With skulls.

I did like the skulls.

Unfortunately the rest was covered with bunched-up netting and a blood-spattered rainbow riot of neon silk flowers that smelled of rancid syrup and mold.

It was a smell an *Amorphophallus titanium* bloom would envy and a look only a Slasher costume designer could love.

Ellen tapped a fingernail on her teeth as she regarded the bulbous padding at the hips. "It would fit in the shoulders."

"I would look like the Queen of Corpse Flowers." I plucked a particularly offensive bright-pink specimen centered where my butt would be.

The flower pulled away from the dress with ease.

I pulled some more, and the dress separated into a satin layer and a mesh net with the flowers attached. "I need scissors."

"Are you sure?"

I held my hand out.

Ten minutes later, the only flowers left were the ones tracing from simple buds and leaves in black on my left shoulder, blooming to a silver rose flecked with garnets and accented by outlines of pomegranates at my waist, and then the flowers faded, wilted and died until all that was left was the shining embroidery of the white skull on the hem.

The matching shoes where white with more pomegranates and skulls outlined in white silk. It was an elegant detail that would probably get missed.

Ellen went to call for a taxi and get her purse while I combed out my curls and tucked them into a chignon. A little hair spray to hold it all in, and the red of my hair went a shade or two darker, matching the garnets better.

Smoky eye makeup, garnet-red lipstick, and when Ellen walked in, she gasped.

I raised an eyebrow. "Well?"

She raised her camera slowly. "Hold still."

"Ellen!"

"The lighting is perfect! Hold still."

I gave her my best Grim Reaper death glare.

"I am going to have the best looking date at this party." Ellen beamed.

"No, I am." I took her arm and smiled. "You look amazing."

Ellen blushed cutely. "Can I keep the photo?"

"Lemme see."

She turned her phone so I could peek at the screen as we walked to the front door and our waiting taxi. The bright makeup lights had washed out the walls in a flood of color and left me standing like Death in a blazing aura of glory.

"Keep it. And send me a copy." I watched her hit send.

"You think I should send one to Morana?"

"And warn him I'm coming? No, let's not ruin his evening." I picked up the skirt and walked to the taxi door feeling like an all-powerful goddess of creation. "Do you think I could get away with wearing this to work?"

"That dress qualifies as a work hazard," Ellen said, opening the taxi door. "You're far too distracting."

I pushed her into the waiting seat. "Get in, gorgeous. You're making me blush."

The cabbie stared at our reflections in the rearview mirror.

"Problem?" I asked.

The cabbie shook her head.

"You have the address?"

The cabbie nodded.

"Can we go?"

"I have sons," the cabbie offered.

I scootched closer to Ellen. "I'm with her."

The cabbie sighed. "You're going to have such beautiful babies."

Ellen smiled up at me. "It's true. We would have beautiful babies."

"It's our first date! Next thing I know you'll be dragging me back to Galena. We could get some acreage by our parents." And I could die of boredom watching the sun set over the Galena River.

"Galena isn't all bad," Ellen said. "I told Patrick about it, and he doesn't think it sounds all bad."

They never did. Small town living was romantic, right up until you had to do it. "You may take Patrick Miles," I said. "I'm staying in Chicago for life."

Somehow I was in the middle of a party, in the middle of the Field Museum, alone.

That was a new skill for me.

Stanley Field Hall had been decorated to match the theme of Lost Things, which was probably just an excuse to use all the winter holiday decorations that hadn't been used for last year's Midwinter Ball because an ice storm had shut down the city for two weeks.

Sharp, glittering snowflakes made of crystal hung overhead, threatening to drop and impale everyone. Pine trees decorated in wintery fair that was not supposed to look specifically religious but still leaned heavily to a twentieth-century European Christmas theme created a curved space.

And amid the greenery, displays of taxidermied animals that had gone extinct skulked with portraits of notable scholars and artists who had died in the past few decades, along with surrealist sculptures made of trash and lost forks.

The overall impression was a winter hellscape as described by someone on a bad acid trip. And the live orchestra from the music department of the local university was playing *The Song Of Ice* from the fantasy RPG I'd played in middle school.

Carefully maneuvering around a cluster of Chicago nouveau riche drenched in overly floral, competing perfumes as they discussed a bent fork with disgusting sincerity, I searched for the purple pop of color in a sea of dull autumnal tones. She was nowhere to be found.

I'd lost Ellen somewhere. How was beyond me. But I had.

Very thematic and all, but troubling. I hoped the curators weren't randomly kidnapping people from the party to maintain the nightmare motif.

Drifting through the crowd, I found a pocket of space away from the greasy smell of the buffet and the dance floor where I could watch most of the room with my back to a support pillar that had escaped the winter wonderland treatment.

"Merri, I didn't expect to see you here." The voice was chilly as the museum air and possibly the best thing I'd heard all night.

"Delilah?" I turned to look at the only woman in Chicago who almost made me envious. She was wearing a blood red Taverly original.[26] Her long, chocolate-brown hair hung in seductive waves down to her hips, and wide, topaz-brown eyes sparkled against flawless, pale skin. And she was a good six inches taller than me. I'd have hated her if we didn't get along so well.

Lifting her champagne glass, Delilah drifted across the floor. "I didn't expect to see you here. Who deserves a dose of Kriesmas Cheer?"

"My friend is making her debut as a film director tonight and I am here as her Plus One and support."

Delilah wrinkled her nose in disappointment. "And here I was hoping for fireworks."

"Sorry to disappoint." I looked around for the person I knew wouldn't be far away.

He wasn't.

Mayor Alan Adale was almost ten years older than me, fair-haired, green-eyed, impossibly fit—and somehow he always managed to stand so the lights hit his cheekbones like they were chiseled. He was beautiful, like a sculpture by Da Vinci or Luo Li Rong. He stepped beside his wife, slid an arm around her waist, and I felt a hot surge of envy for the look they shared.

I rolled my eyes. "How long have you been married?"

---

[26] The dress had been hot gossip for weeks.

"Nine years in January," the mayor said without missing a beat.

"It would have been sooner if I'd actually shown up to our first date." Delilah rested her head on her husband's shoulder. "But that's ancient history. Merri was just telling me about her friend who is a film director?" Delilah raised an elegantly sculpted eyebrow. "But first, I have to know about the dress. I don't think we've ever seen you in this style."

Sleek and skin tight? No, I couldn't remember the last time I'd worn anything like it either. I lifted my glass. "Thank the costume department at Cozy Studios. This was a last-minute affair."

Delilah chuckled.

The mayor's eye caught on someone and he whispered something to his wife.

She looked past me with an appraising smile. "Remember the old cartoon where Hades is played by a guy with blue flames for hair?"

"I think I've seen some of the memes." At the Museum of Contemporary Art of Chicago, about three miles north of where we were. "Why?"

"The man who could play him in the live-action movie just arrived. Hades is here and..." Delilah tipped her chin to the side as she studied my dress. The pomegranates. The flowers. The embroidered skull. She smirked.

I smiled sweetly back at her.

"He looks familiar," Adale said.

Since there was no polite way to ignore the conversation at this point, I looked over my shoulder and saw Seth: a sleek, dark silver button-down shirt that absorbed the light, tailored black slacks that hinted at the body underneath, platinum white hair artfully tousled. The lights played across the sharp angles of his face, flirting with shadows, caressing his lips the way I'd wanted to more than once this afternoon. Mayor Adale was not the best looking man in the room.

"You know him?" Delilah guessed in her very best confessional tone. People liked to talk to Delilah, spill their secrets, share their burdens.

I'd never been very good at sharing. "I know his name. Seth Morana, head of the Slasher–Cozy Studios. I've bumped into him before." I turned back to the political couple with a smile. "You've probably seen him on screen before."

Adale and Delilah shared a look but both shook their heads.

"So," Delilah said in the drawn-out way of someone stalling for time, "what have you been up to since we spoke last? I heard the case at Windy City Security wrapped early. Are you planning another trip? Miami, perhaps?"

"Ah." I chuckled in mild embarrassment. "You called the art dealer I told you about?"

"Mister Kane[27] was very helpful," Delilah said. "Very

---

[27] My gem expert. Rafael Kane was the reason I knew a fake opal when I spotted one. We'd met years ago while stuck in the Atlanta Airport and had bonded over reruns of *Timberwolf Town*, spotting fake gems on first class passengers, and drinking tiny bottles of rum.

complimentary of you as well."

"And very engaged, as of January." The wedding invite had sent my office into a tizzy of speculation. They were so used to my hate mail that the idea someone was inviting me to an event because we were—nominally—friends was quite confusing.

I suspect the invite had more to do with the fact that Del Farmer, Kane's bride-to-be, was nearly as efficient and organized as I was and there was a sizable wedding budget, so everyone they knew was invited.

My plan to go was motivated purely by mercenary reasons: the couple both worked for one of the best art houses in the country and the guest list would include many new, lucrative, clients for Sloan and Markham. The best kind of beach vacations were the ones where I spent the entire time adding up dollar signs.[28]

"Merri!" My name, gasped in a deep and unfamiliar tenor, grabbed my attention.

I turned, saw a blue shirt, and looked up, up, up, into the hazel eyes of Patrick Miles. Cue the confusion. "Patrick."

He tugged one of the decorative pines to fill a gap that exposed our bubble to the rabble and slumped against the column I'd been hiding behind. He took a breath, and then rebuilt himself.

"Are you okay?" Delilah asked, looking him over.

Patrick shook his head. Somehow he managed to look boyishly charming and scandalously handsome in the same movement. I could see why Ellen liked him.

---

[28] And avoiding cartels. But that's another story.

"It's just…" Patrick shook his head. "Mild, mild social anxiety."

"I know that one," the mayor murmured. "If I could, I'd ghost right out of here." His eyes lit up with amusement at some private joke as his wife shook her head.

"Ellen said that if I couldn't find her, I could come to you." Patrick looked at me pleadingly.

I smiled back. "I'm happy to be your human shield until we find Ellen again."

"Thank you," he said with enough gratitude I almost felt bad for him. "This is why I left Hollywood. I couldn't do the crowds any more. People pawing at me, grabbing me and photographing me, and acting like they owned me because I was in the public eye. I thought Cozy would be safe."

"If anyone gives you trouble Merri can't handle, we'll help," Delilah said.

"Time for introductions," I said before Patrick accidentally got sucked into the black mires of Chicago politics. I understood wanting a breather from the sycophants here to boost their social media numbers by chasing the elusive status of Celebrity, but he should know who he was dealing with first. "Mayor Adale, Delilah Samson, VP of Subrosa Security, this is Patrick Miles. He's starring in a new Cozy holiday movie."

"*Winter Wish*," Patrick said with the charming smile of someone who had been marketing movies since he was twelve. "It's going to be phenomenal. You couldn't ask for a better cast or crew. The story is—"

I patted his arm. "They don't care."

The mayor chuckled. "Miss Kriesmas is too blunt.

We care. I'm sure the movie will be wonderful and we're happy to have Cozy Studios in Chicago doing well." His smile was picture perfect, but it never touched his eyes. The mayor cared about the money Slasher and Cozy brought to the city, but nothing more.

That was fine. Trying to picture Delilah curled up watching a Cozy romance made my head spin. Some things were just not meant to be.

Behind the mayor, a man with a teal tie appeared, searching for someone with increasing desperation.

"Delilah, the man in the green tie—"

She closed her eyes in resignation. "Intern for a lobbyist. Alan's almost done with his second term as mayor and there's a push for him to move to the state level. Or national. We've been dodging them all evening."

"Do you need me to run interference?" I couldn't magic away Delilah's political problems, but she was a friend of sorts. She'd helped me when I'd arrived in Chicago, made sure the worst of the pictures of me were scrubbed from everywhere on the internet,[29] and had given me a mentor-figure, if not a friend.

"If I need help from Chicago's favorite Grim Reaper, I'll give you a call. But for now"—Delilah glanced back at the crowd—"I think we'll stick to our script."

"I can now say no in over thirty languages," the mayor said with only a hint of a laugh. "I'm not leaving Chicago any time soon."

"Good luck," I said, lifting my glass. "Scream if you need me."

---

[29] I'm still not sure how.

Delilah winked as she and her husband turned, bearing down on the helpless teal-tied fool with all the weight of Chicago behind them.

"Fun couple," Patrick said in a slow, careful way. "Grim Reaper. Is that a street name? Or nickname? Or did you just plot murder with the mayor?"

"Only as a joke." Mostly as a joke. "The kind of damage I'd do would all be financial. I don't actually *kill*-kill people. Just their careers. And reputations. And hidden slush funds."

I loved finding hidden slush funds. The screams of trust-fund children realizing that they wouldn't be inheriting Mommy and Daddy's ill-gotten loot are delicious.

"You're terrifying," Patrick said.

"Ellen didn't really prep you for this introduction, did she?" I finally gave him my full attention.

Patrick Miles was a generic white American actor: tall, fit, good hair, nice smile. He looked like the other thousand or so actors hired every year because he fit the current definition of masculine beauty and gave the general impression of being slightly smarter than a doorknob.

I narrowed my eyes, trying to divine why Ellen— sweet, loveable, innocent Ellen—would throw Patrick Miles to a monster like me. Did she *want* me to destroy him? I knew she couldn't think I'd like him.

Patrick's smile wavered under my scrutiny. "Ellen told me you were her best friend and that you'd handle anything if I couldn't find her. What else did I need to know?"

"Nothing, I suppose." I changed my smile to warm and friendly. Seth might have noticed the tension in my jaw or the glare in my eye. Patrick missed it. Or didn't care. "What are you up to tonight?"

"Trying desperately to remember how to interact with people."

One of the waitstaff passed with a tray full of drinks and Patrick grabbed one, knocked it back in a single, panicked gulp, and put the empty glass back on the tray.

"I've been up at my ranch in Wyoming since September. We, ah, provide emergency medical care for the wild horses. It's great if you love wide open vistas."

Oh dear heavens, I was going to kill someone in public.

That would ruin the hem of my dress. And then Ellen would pout. Where was Ellen?

I scanned the crowd as Patrick droned on about horses.

Black tuxes.

Bright pink hair, that was Alisson.

Lots of red dresses.

Plenty of blues and greens.

Where the flippity-flopping-fluffy-tailed duck was Ellen?

A small group of socialites in towering, spiked heels and elegantly manicured hands parted and I saw Ellen in the middle, looking down at everyone's chins and twisting her skirt around her fingers like she did before every school play. Someone had scared Ellen.

Okay, well that cleared up my evening's To Do list. People *were* going to die.

Patrick froze midsentence. "Are you okay?"

"I'm fine," I said in a perfectly polite tone as my jaw clenched.

"You went very still. And cold." He cleared his throat nervously. "Is—is there an ex over there?" He turned, trying to see what I was looking at.

"Patrick," I drew his name out as I ticked through my options, "what do you think of Ellen?"

"She's amazing!" It was such an enthusiastic response I took a split second to look at his face and make sure he wasn't lying. His smile was Oscar-worthy. "I love working with her. She's so generous on set. So clear with what she wants and what she needs with us. Best director I've ever had."

"Good. So, you'd be willing to help Ellen?"

He beamed. "Of course!"

Excellent. I smiled.

Somewhere, the king of Hell trembled in fear.

"Here's the plan. I'm going to walk over and break up the flock of vultures currently trying eat Ellen alive. It'll be enough to get them to step back. Let Ellen answer two questions, and then show up with a drink for her and— this is the important part—eyes only for her. You are going to spend the rest of the night pretending Ellen is the only other person at this party. You two are getting your own little pocket universe."

"Sounds perfect."

Again, I had to look up to see his face.

Patrick was smiling softly as he watched Ellen, completely entranced.

Surreptitiously, I sniffed the wine in my glass. It didn't smell drugged.

I felt fine. It was just the rest of the universe that was being weird. Sure, the Hollywood Hunk had a crush on the sweet little Black girl from Galen, Illinois.

The Cozy Curse was strong.

A shiver of disgust ran up my back. I had to get Seth's accounts wrapped up and passed off before someone tried to convince me to tour suburbia with him, or live on a horse ranch. I side-eyed Patrick hard, finished my probably-not-tainted wine, and set the glass on a passing tray.

"You ready?"

"Always ready," Patrick said.

I put on a dazzling smile that would make the sun sink in shame, and strutted into the center of everything like I could make the world spin around me.

I drew attention like I was owed it in my contract.

I made heads turn like it was my job.

The sheer social force of my advance was enough to slam into the socialites and knock them all back with belligerent frowns. They huffed, exchanging whispered remarks as they tried to identify me and regroup.

But it was far, far too late for that.

Like the last rays of the sun before a final solar flare ripped apart the planet, I brightened. "Ellen!" I took her arm. "There you are. I've been looking all over for you." Leaning back to cut off the first counter-attack, I looked at her outfit. "I love this dress on you! The purple is your color. Ever the empress." I gave her a quick air kiss.

Ellen's eyes went wide in confusion and surprise. "Hello to you too."

"Why don't you introduce me to your friends?" I held her hand and snuggled close to her shoulder. The extra height of my heels didn't get me on the same level as the gatekeepers of Chicago's high society, but it gave me almost an inch over Ellen and enough leverage to bring them down to my level.

"We're not exactly friends," Ellen said in the strained yet polite tone that had signaled she was overwhelmed, unconfident, and surrounded by ferals ever since second grade when Olivia Watkins had taken her friendship bracelet back and publicly uninvited Ellen from her birthday party because she didn't like Ellen having the same backpack as her.

If there'd been a soundtrack, the fight music would have started playing.

Instead we got the orchestral arrangement playing something light, and airy, and probably composed for another RPG from the early twenty-first century, with a background addition of rainforest sounds.

The occasional scream from a fake macaw really set the tone.

The lead vulture stepped forward, her blonde hair moving as a set piece. "Kandace Arbutum, Arbutum Financial."

Ellen's worried expression turned to a small, knowing smile. My best friend had seen this drama play out before and she knew how it was going to end.

Miss Arbutum, alas, did not know she was about to be destroyed. "I'm sure you have a reason for not knowing me," Kandace said with sarcastic smugness that made her friends titter in amusement.

Ooo. Scary. Shots fired.

I didn't roll my eyes because my mama brought me up better than that. But, really, if Kandace wanted to bring the thunder, she needed better than ammo than that.

"Merri Kriesmas," I said with a smile as I unsnapped my clutch and held out a card. "When your company moves to the big leagues, give me a call."

A quick cough covered Ellen's laugh as she suddenly found her shoes fascinating beyond compare.

Kandace took the card and fell back, taking two of the other vultures with her. Three down, five to go.

"Kriesmas?" An intelligent-looking brunette smiled down at me. "Chicago's own Wicked Witch."

It took me a minute to place her face. "Bexley Bekstrum, of Bekstrum Realty? And how is your brother?"

Her artificially plumped lips zipped into a thin, angry line.

"It's good your family wears orange so well."

"Merri!" Ellen pinched my arm.

"Oh, fine, I'll play nice," I promised her. "I assume they all came to see who the new girl on the playground was?"

"We were introducing Miss Berry to some of the finer points of Chicago society," said a woman with naturally tanned skin, dark brown hair, and the faintest hint of a Manhattan accent. Her jade-green dress was two seasons out of style, but her shoes were from the

Ligantii fall line, shimmering, liquid gold.[30]

I smiled at Miss Manhattan. "It's rather silly to tell a trendsetter what's in fashion. You should be asking."

The gaggle scoffed.

"She's not a trendsetter," Miss Manhattan said.

"Ellen." I smiled. "What's everyone going to be wearing for New Year's?"

I knew my friend well. She closed her eyes as she mentally cataloged what Cozy was offering. "Periwinkle satin will be the must-have item of the year, paired with emeralds and gold. Ultramarine and silver are the hot colors for winter weddings. Shoes will be"—she glanced at Miss Manhattan's feet—"not those atrocities."

"I like them," I whispered.

"You have terrible taste in shoes," Ellen said, not quite quietly enough to be missed. Louder, she continued, "Holiday wear will be winter pastels, red is out, and cold whites are in. Also look for stunning, metallic blacks. The Little Black Dress is going to be overshadowed by the Long Black Dress for all sizes and shapes before Thanksgiving."

I looked at the mob's array of autumn colors. In April, no less. And I smirked. A well-placed smirk can do wonders.

Just before I verbally eviscerated their egos, Patrick called out. "Ellen!" He showed up like a knight in a shining, seasonally appropriate, three-pieced suit.

---

[30] Guess who did some work for Chicago fashion week and kinda got hooked on shoes? Did you guess me? It was me.

"Ellen..." Patrick took a breath as he looked her up and down, eyes widening in appreciation. "You look amazing."

"Oh." Ellen's blush ran up her cheeks to her ears. "Thank you."

A dainty, white hand with bold blue nail polish reached for Patrick.

"Excuse me, are you Patrick Miles?"

Clearly I hadn't done my job as Grim Reaper well enough, because one of Bexley's entourage was sizing the movie star up like a sushi dinner. I shouldn't have worn white shoes; the blood stains were going to show.

"There's the cute couple." Alisson sauntered in wearing an angular black leather crop top and a flowing black skirt that would have looked terrible on me but only accented Alisson's feminine beauty. Even her spiky pink hair looked effortless flawless. Not that I was jealous.[31] "Ellen, Patrick's been looking all over for you." She leaned in to give Ellen air kisses over her cheeks and stab Miss Blue with a look that promised a slow, painful death.

"Oh?" Ellen looked up at Patrick with a worried, adoring expression that made her absolutely precious. Ugh. I'd forgotten how adorable my friend was. If Patrick didn't make a move, he was a fool. "I thought you weren't coming until later."

"I showed up a little early so I could see you."

Patrick's smile was going to make Cozy so much money come December.

---

[31] Much.

Alisson sighed as she lifted her champagne glass to her lips. "Ah. Love."

"You could call my sister," I reminded her.

The socialites were wavering, torn between trying to get the attention of Patrick—who was playing his role of devoted boyfriend to perfection—and the very sensible urge to run away from Alisson and me.

My future sister-in-law was studying me. "This is a good look for you."

"Thanks. It is."

Behind us the music changed to a waltz. I saw the Delilah and the mayor moving onto the dance floor and other couples followed.

"Do you dance?" I asked Alisson.

"Not with you." She gave me an enigmatic look. "Seth and I have a strict No Poaching rule."

"Seth's not around." I hadn't seen him since he'd entered, and I needed a reason to step away from Ellen and Patrick asap. If Ellen had another Plus One, I was free to go home to my sorely missed bed.

A dark shadow fell across me with the scent of sandalwood soap. "Who's not around?" Seth winked at Alisson, who rolled her eyes. "I almost missed you, Red Hot." He slipped his arm around my waist and pulled me close with a smolder that was hot enough to start the second great Chicago fire.

Good googly-moogly, I'd thought I known what a well-fitted black suit looked like before, but I'd been sorely, sinfully mistaken. I took a half-step back so I could appreciate the pure art of the dark silver shirt that hugged Seth like a lover, and the shadowy black jacket and pants that fit him as if tailored by God himself. Seth was breathtaking… and color coordinated with me like we'd planned it.

If I didn't have the full focus of the would-be queens of Chicago before, I did now. Patrick Miles was generically handsome. Seth Morana was striking, charismatic, and drop-dead gorgeous. And right now his dark eyes were focused on me.

"Do you dance?" Seth asked.

"With you? Yes." Anyone else would have had their arm broken by now.

Seth looked around, not at the socialites, but at the crowds beyond them. "You sure? The news sites all have drones, and the event's people are taking photos. We can go find a corner to lurk in if you want."

Faceless photos on Seth's social media was one thing; full pictures were something altogether different. I'd be seen.

Without my brightly colored armor.

Without layers of work for insulation.

Without filters, or fades, or hidden face shots.

With Seth.

I smiled. "Let's go dance."

We swayed in three-four time, the music leading the assembly in slow circles.

"You're glaring," Seth whispered as we made another loop past the buffet table. "That's not usually the reception I get."

I shot him a quick glare. "I'm trying to keep track of Ellen."

"Mmm." Seth deftly turned us around so I could have a full view of my friend in the center of a growing pool of people captivated by Patrick's smile. "She's fine. Alisson is on stand-by to swoop in if either of them need rescuing."

"Did you know Patrick doesn't like crowds?"

"Ellen brought it up when I suggested the cast coming tonight. We were going to make an excuse for him, but he said he'd be fine if Ellen were here."

I glowered at the actor. "He latched onto her fast. If he hurts Ellen—"

"I will personally burn his career to ash," Seth promised.

"You say the sweetest things." I smiled up at him and forgot about friends, actors, and crowds for a moment. His dark eyes were warm and soft. "And you are an amazing actor. You play the role of devoted boyfriend perfectly."

In his arms, I felt like I could breathe again. Shed a layer of armor. Steal a moment of happiness.

Right. Happiness.

That's what I was planning to steal from Seth. Not a kiss.

Not a *single* kiss.

Maybe a lot of kisses though.

Seth smiled like he could read my thoughts. Taking my hand, he led us off the dance floor as the music changed to another insipid holiday song. He slowed next to a table, but then kept going, leading me away from the noise and to a quiet, dark hall where the only sound was our heavy breathing.

The wall at my back was cool and smooth. It felt like the only solid thing in the room. My whole body was burning with need. It had been so, so long since I wanted anyone this much. Wanted to feel their skin against mine. Wanted to be wanted. I licked my lips and tried to come back to reality; not exactly an easy task with Seth leaning over me, arm braced against the wall.

His eyes were dark and hungry and I wanted everything his look promised.

If only. "You don't need to act tonight." The words came out breathier than I'd planned. I had to give him the out. Had to break this spell before he broke me.

"I'm not acting." His voice was low and tantalizing. "I'm behaving. This is an exercise in impulse control."

"Really?" Hope was such a delicate thing before, and now it felt like a monster that might destroy my heart.

Seth came closer, lips almost on mine. "What I want might be more PDA than you're comfortable with."

I smiled, gripping the lapels of his jacket. "Really?"

His smile grew to match mine. "That's... not the look of a woman who is objecting."

"It's really, really not." I brushed a thumb along the thin fabric of his shirt.

"Really?" His hand slid down the wall and landed gently on my waist.

Did I want him to pin me to the wall like a piece of fine art?

Yes.

Definitely yes.

Please, dear universe, yes. I'd never wanted anything as much as I wanted Seth to kiss me. Time had frozen, the world could end, and still all that would matter was us.

"You're beautiful." Seth lips were a breath away.

My eyes fluttered shut in anticipation.

My phone rang in my pocket.

Seth froze because he had good instincts and better self-control than I did.

The phone rang again, the opening bars of the soundtrack to *Black and Blue*, the critically acclaimed, award-winning film about the race wars of the early twenty-first century.

"It's the police," I muttered as I reached for my pocket. If it wasn't urgent, I was going to murder someone; at least then they'd have a reason to talk to me.

Seth stepped away. "You have a special ring tone for the police?"

"Yes." I slid the answer button to green. "They're frequent clients." I held the phone to my ear. "This better be good."

"Happy holidays to you too, Merri Kriesmas," said a deep tenor voice with the wisp of sarcasm and a Jersey accent.

"Dan, why are you calling?"

There was a snicker on the other end of the line. "Basic courtesy call is all. We've had a couple of noise complaints from your apartment. A lot of banging and thumping." He made it sound dirty.

I looked up at Seth and then down the hall. "Detective, I'm not home. I'm at the city art festival at the Field Museum."

Seth tilted his head.

I held up a finger and stepped away.

"You sure?" Dan sounded skeptical.

"Absolutely positive." I walked to the entrance of the hall and looked out across the assembly. "Would you like to ask the chief of police or Mayor Adale? I can see them both from where I'm standing." I could also see my shot to kiss Seth Morana riding off into the sunset. Flirtation was lovely, but the reality was that my work hours were not nine to five. No sane person wanted that schedule.

Warm air behind me was the first hint Seth had stepped closer. Then his hand stroked my bare arm. "Is everything okay?"

I nodded tensely. Holding my phone down by my hip I gave him a quick smile. "I'm just going to step out for a minute. Can you grab my purse from the coat check? Ellen has our tickets. I might have to run home real quick."

"I'll go get your purse," Seth said, his fingers lingering against mine. With a quick squeeze and a sad smile, Seth stepped away.

Lifting the phone back to my ear, I sighed. "I was in a crowd. Let me get outside while you explain what's happening."

"It's a noise complaint." On the other end of the phone, Dan cleared his throat. "Do you have a cat? New puppy?"

"I don't keep pets." My teeth ground together as I took a side exit to the deck overlooking Lake Shore Drive. "Detective, you have my permission to go into my apartment and see what the fuss is about. I'll let the building security know you'll be there in under five minutes." It was an order and we both knew it.

We also both knew Dan would get someone there in under five minutes because I'd brought the Chicago PD the evidence to close multiple high-profile cases.

There wasn't anything in my apartment, but criminals didn't know that. If they wanted to destroy evidence or get revenge, attacking my apartment made sense. Especially since I was supposed to be home tonight.

Taking a deep breath, I hung up on Dan and dialed the building security office.

"This is Vinny at—"

"Vinny, it's Merri from apartment eight twenty-nine. The police informed me there was a noise complaint."

"Yes, Miss." Vinny was an older man with wiry gray haircut like an army recruit. He'd been at the building when I moved in and would probably be there when I finally died and they dragged my cold corpse out. "I hate to complain, Miss, but you're making a racket."

"Vinny, I'm not home." I paused to let that sink in. "Detective Dan Park is on his way to check it out. Lock down the elevators and the fire doors to the stairs."

"Yes, Miss." Vinny coughed. "The cameras on your floor blinked out but they'ze just come back on, Miss. Your door is broken something awful." Another cough. "The building is locked down now. But I think they might already be out."

"Fantastic," I said sarcastically. "Did any visitors sign in?"

"Nope. Everyone who came in this evening had a key and headed straight up to their apartments."

Not very comforting. "All right."

"The police are here," Vinny reported.

"Give them full access to my apartment," I said. "Tell them I want photos. I'll be there in about twenty minutes."

"All rig—No. The uniform is shaking her head no. They say they'll call," Vinny said.

"Fine." Not fine. I didn't want to sit here waiting to hear what had happened. I hung up with a scowl. This wasn't how I'd pictured my evening going.

Granted, I hadn't really had a plan other than Support Ellen, and maybe Flirt With Seth. But there was definitely no Get Burgled on the agenda.

The parking lot was full but there was probably a cab down at the corner. I stepped off the deck down to the curb, trying to get a good view of the street past the maples, wondering if I could walk or if I'd need to call for a ride as a sedan roared past, hitting the one remaining puddle in the street and splashing me with a sluice of dirty water.

"Mer—" Seth ran up beside me. "—ri. Oh, boy."

Gravel and filthy water clung to the white skirt. "Ellen is not going to be happy."

"It's not the worst thing the dress has seen," Seth said in what he probably thought was a soothing tone. "What was the call about? Or is there an NDA in place?" He tried to pass it off as a joke, but it wasn't; he was worried.

I smiled brightly. "Someone broke into my apartment."

Seth had never looked terrifying before.

Cute. Sweet. Hot. Even devilishly handsome in a few of his portraits. Now he looked like the monster he played in movies. "Are you going home?"

"Not yet. They said they'll call, so—" I stopped as I opened my purse and looked at my little hot-pink wallet. It wasn't snapped shut. That was bizarre. Lifting it out of my clutch, I flipped it open.

My building card and ID were both missing. Along with my bank card.

"Is everything okay?"

"Grand." I showed him my wallet. "No ID. No bank card. No way to go home. No way I'm getting out of tonight without hours of teasing and a phone call from both my parents on Sunday when my parents are participating in the twenty-first century."

"Teasing?" Seth raised his eyebrows.

I shrugged. "I have to call my sister? Lucky's the only one who's going to come take care of me." Waking up my phone, I checked the time and groaned. "And she's at roller derby for another three hours. I guess I'll go find a washroom and see what I can do to fix this dress with paper towels."

"It's an emergency," Seth said. "I'm sure your sister will drop everything for you."

That made me laugh. "No, she wouldn't. And regardless, I won't call her before she's done."

"Why not?"

"Because she's got another hour until her game down in Champaign, so even if she could drop everything, she drove and would need to take three of the other team members out of the game to go home, because they carpooled, and she wouldn't be here anytime soon."

Seth narrowed his eyes. "But she'd do it. I can't picture your sister getting upset over a phone call."

"But I would be," I said fixing on my largest smile. "I just—"

My phone rang again.

This time, I stayed close to Seth as I answered. "Hello, Dan."

"Hey, so, your house looks like it got hit by a tornado. Not what I was expecting. Your TV is missing."

"I don't own a TV."

"Computer?"

"I have a work laptop, nothing else."

"Did you have anything of value in this apartment?" Dan asked.

I thought about it. "My dress collection? My cooking pots are worth a few hundred? I think my sister left some old Scotch in one of the cupboards, but I'm not sure."

"Merri," Dan said with annoyance, "do you actually own anything that a robber would want?"

"Sure. But I keep it in the company safe, not at my apartment."

Seth was watching me curiously.

I shrugged. "Can I head home now?"

"You should probably get a hotel room for the night," Dan said. "The windows are broken and the front lock is busted. Your security guy says they can have it fixed by Monday."

"By Monday?" I sighed. "Sure. Fine."

"You got a change of clothes somewhere?"

"A couple of dresses at the dry cleaner." Clean underthings in my spare gym bag in the trunk of my car, still parked over at Slasher studios. "I'll be fine. Do you need me for anything tonight?"

"No. We'll schedule a walk-through tomorrow. Probably around ten or eleven. Does that work?"

"Sure." It wasn't like I had a choice.

"Keep your phone on," Dan said. "Call me right away if anything else happens tonight."

I frowned. "Like what?"

"People following you. Strange cars. You know the drill. We didn't find anyone here, which means they might go after you."

My smile was tight. "Don't worry. I'm in a very public place with excellent security. I'll be fine."

"Don't walk to the hotel." Detective Park knew me a little too well.

"I'll take that under advisement."

"I'm serious, Merri. You need to be careful until we know what they were looking for."

"It's an apartment on the expensive end of town and they probably saw the lights were off and decided to go grab my jewelry collection," I said in exasperation. "It's not like the local burglars know I don't have anything worth stealing. I'm one of three apartments in the building with no additional digital security."

"You should get some," Dan said.

"I like my privacy and I've seen too many cases of hacked security cameras. Thanks."

Dan made a grumbling sound that could have been an insult, but I didn't catch enough to hear. "Get to the hotel. Lock the door. Stay put until I call you in the morning."

"Right. Goodnight." I hung up. That wasn't going to happen. "What day is it?" I asked Seth.

"Still Friday."

"I don't want to deal with this right now." With another sigh, I closed my eyes and tried to find the layers of armor I needed to deal with the people inside. "I don't want to deal with family right now. Or nagging. Or people. Or anything else, actually. I want to go home, but I can't, so I'm going to go fix this dress, go back to the ballroom, and make it through the rest of the night."

"Come home with me," Seth said, holding out his hand. "Clean shower. Your choice of t-shirts that will be too large with you. Whatever I can scrounge from the fridge. No nagging, family, or random people."

That was a very tempting offer. My resolve wavered. It would be so easy, so very easy, to throw my problems away for the night and let Seth take care of me. To pretend we were ordinary people for a few hours. To lie and say we weren't both carrying scars.

I faked a cheerful smile. "No family drama? Pretty sure this is how Persephone seduced Hades."

"Didn't Hades kidnap Persephone?" Seth took a step closer.

"Absolutely not. You think the quiet, geek king of the underworld was going to kidnap the OG maiden goddess? His special thing was being invisible, while she was the goddess of renewal, rebirth, and second chances. Poor boy didn't even know what hit him."

Seth licked his lips and curled around me. "Is that how the story goes?"

"Most certainly." I could feel his breath on my neck. One little move and his lips... Hmmm. I leaned into him as I looked up at the heavy clouds overhead.

When I was seven, I'd won the Miss Sunshine contest at the county fair and someone had left a dead snake on my doorstep with the note *Your Next*. My first death threat, bad spelling and all.

At seventeen, a boy I thought I loved tried to steal my future. He'd stolen my image, and my name, and my sense of security. He'd taken everything I loved about myself and sold it to the highest bidder.

I wanted it back.

I wanted my whole life back. I was done analyzing every show of affection for the hint of deceit. I was done holding everyone at arm's length because I couldn't risk being hurt again.

I genuinely liked Seth. I liked how he treated me, and how he made me laugh. I liked this moment together wrapped in sandalwood and retreating storms.

"How about these two reapers call it a night and go home?" Seth whispered.

It was time to move forward with my life, to let my guard down just a little, and try this whole dating thing again. Even if started with a wedding proposal under some mistletoe.

I snuggled closer to Seth. "A before-breakfast rendezvous, ring shopping after lunch, and an invite home? You need to be careful, Mister Morana, or you're going to kill your Hollywood Playboy reputation."

"Mister Morana?" He chuckled. "I don't suppose that amazing dress collection of yours includes a pencil skirt."

"It might," I teased.

It didn't. Yet. I could fix that.

With a quick kiss on the cheek, Seth pulled away, taking my hand. "Let's go home, Killer."

Hot, sandalwood-scented steam from the shower curled around my legs and chased me through the chill of Seth's darkened bedroom. The walk-in closet was next to a vanity with a three-way mirror that fit the neighborhood but not the person living in the house. It was hard to imagine him stopping to check if his uncombed hair was rumbled sexily enough or his oversized hoodie hung just so before leaving for work each day.

On the other hand, it was very easy to picture other things some*ones* might do with a mirror like that in the bedroom. I peeked over my shoulder to see where the bed was. Despite expectations, all that could be seen from the alcove of the vanity was the door to the living room and the windows.

A little bit of oversight on the designer's part. Someone had lacked imagination.

I was also fairly certain I'd seen a promo shot of a horror movie with a mirror like this at the studio, and it wouldn't surprise me in the least to find out Seth bought this apartment with set design in mind.

Seth's apartment was made of stone and concrete with dark, hardwood floors and views of the Chicago skyline to the south. There were fluted columns and huge, industrial-sized windows that made even Seth look small.

In the darkness as a storm swirled outside, it was easy to imagine I'd wandered into the Underworld.

A cozy underworld with a closet filled with black shirts and hoodies, an elusive suit or two, and the occasional white dress shirt. I picked one and shrugged it on.

"You should wear something else," Seth said.

I frowned at the empty room behind me. His voice had the odd quality of an echo off concrete walls, but I couldn't see him anywhere. "Do you have a camera?"

"I have a reflection on the patio glass." There was a smirk in his voice. "That shirt turns translucent if it gets wet."

"Interesting…" I looked back to the mirror and, sure enough, where my wet hair had dropped on the shirt, my skin was perfectly visible without even a tint of foggy color from the fabric. "And you don't want me to wear it?"

"Not tonight."

"If you say so."

Nodding at how reasonable—if unfortunately un-sexy—it sounded, I dove back into the closet looking for something soft, long, and not see-through.

At the end of a long row of fading black t-shirts, I found one with the peeling red Slasher™ font spelling out the words 'Killer Lookz'. It was soft as silk and hung to mid-thigh, covering more skin than most of my swimwear.

I took the vanishing dress shirt with me.

Funny, his kiss at the museum had definitely felt like a *yes, tonight,* sort of kiss. For most other people it would have been more flirtation in the car, fumbling through door as we kissed, and a short-lived fling on the bed. The shower was usually the end of the night, not the first thing my date suggested.

I walked through the hall between Seth's bedroom and the kitchen, looking at the pictures on the wall. One by one, people vanished from his life. There were pictures from his teens. A picture cut from a newspaper of him and four other boys standing next to a university sign, holding a trophy. The names Seth, Michael, Liam, and Mason were there, except Michael's had been crossed off with a red pen and the name Alisson was written in a familiar hand.

Seth stood at the end of the hall, watching me.

"Alisson looks good with her hair long," I said, since he seemed to expect some comment, and then moved on to more pictures of Seth with friends. Seth with co-stars. Seth on the red carpet and caught by paparazzi.

Very few faces showed up more than once.

The smell of caramelizing onions overpowered the lingering smell of the shower and Seth's soap. "You made dinner?" If that wasn't an opening, I'd turn in my Prada heels.

"I reheated some risotto," Seth said, stepping back into the kitchen and pulling a pair of black bowls from the microwave.

Holding up the magically sexy shirt, I waited until he turned before making it do a little dance in front of me.

He raised an eyebrow.

I smiled. "It's comfy. I might wear it later."

"Really?"

Tossing the shirt on the back of the couch, I nodded. "Invisible shirts have many uses."

"Mmm." He put the bowls on the table. "What do you want to drink? Beer? Wine? Something stronger? Water?"

"Strong sounds great, but I probably should stick to water."

"Water it is." He filled a glass for me and then started filling a second.

"You can drink whatever you want, I don't mind."

Dark eyes went to the shirt on the couch and the oversized tee I was wearing. "Water is probably best."

"Maybe," I said, with a healthy layer of skepticism.

"Too many late nights in a row can lead to mistakes."

Right. Seth was being cautious. I sat down at the head of the dining table, back to the windows, and inspected the contents of the bowl.

"Mushroom risotto," Seth said, sliding my glass of water toward me. "The catering company does a good job with it and it reheats well." He frowned a little as he sat beside me. "You don't have to eat if you're not hungry. Nibbling at the buffet wasn't enough for me and didn't want to be rude. I know some people don't eat after nine or whatever."

"Some people also keep normal hours," I said, picking up my spoon with a smile.

His whole demeanor was starting to worry me. Earlier, he'd been flirtatious, confident, and fun. But since I'd arrived at his house, it was like he was bracing for impact.

I considered the possibility that he was responsible for the burglar in my apartment—and dismissed it just as quickly. If he'd done anything to maneuver me to his house tonight, he would have followed through. Instead he was just eating. In silence. Watching me like an abused puppy who was waiting for a shoe to get thrown at him.

Taking a bite of the risotto, I looked around as it slowly dawned on me: the big, bad Slasher CEO was scared I was going to reject him. He of the sexily tousled hair, and perfect suit, and stunning abs was worried he wasn't good enough for me.

Sure, I was the Wicked Witch of the South Side and struck terror into the hearts of everyone around me, but only as my day job.

And, yes, I suppose it was fair to argue that I was not really into long-term relationships, but I'd made my decision when I came home with Seth.

This little Miss Kriesmas was going to get herself a second date.

I tossed my regrettably still-wet hair and hit him with a dazzling smile that had dropped more than one person to their knees. "So… you let a Grim Reaper into your house."

"Oh no. Whatever shall I do?" The corner of his mouth crooked up in a mocking smile.

"Mmm, it's big trouble. Something's going to die tonight." I made a show of looking around for house plants or art. There were a few pieces from his movies, but no plants.

Seth took another bite of risotto without looking bothered. "You gonna kill the lights?"

"No, but I think your reputation as a love 'em and leave 'em player is DOA." I leaned closer, angling my body and letting my knee brush his. "A real player would have let me wear that shirt to dinner."

His eyes went wide as he considered the possibilities. Then he shook his head. "Maybe I'm just playing with you. Or maybe I already had my fun for tonight. There were lots of beautiful women at the party." He waited for me to finish the last bite of my risotto and took our bowls away.

"Were there other women there tonight?" I asked, chasing after him. "Describe one of them. Ow!"

The *ow* was because I had stubbed my pinky toe on the small step between the dining area and kitchen.

Seth dropped the bowls in the sink with a clatter and rushed to me. "Are you okay?"

"Yeah, fine, just unable to walk, apparently." I lifted my foot up to rub my toe. "Don't mind me." Of all the idiotic, ridiculous ways to injure myself. Yup. Stubbed toe. As if I hadn't been walking since I was eight months old.

"Here." He scooped me up as if I weighed nothing. "How bad is it?"

"Just a little stub," I protested—but not to being picked up. The man had *muscle* and I was happy to be cradled in his arms as he carried me bridal style into the bedroom.

The guest bedroom.

I sulked as he dropped me onto the bed.

"Can I look at it?" Seth's hand hovered over my foot.

"Go for it." I propped myself up on my elbows and watched as he gently lifted my foot and checked for scrapes, bruises, jutting bone, or severed toes. My toe was fine, but I let him explore anyway.

He brushed away a speck of dust and looked at me, worry in his eyes. "Does it hurt?"

"My whole foot is a little sore…" I mean, what sane person was going to tell Seth Morana to stop touching them?

Seth blushed and looked down at the bedspread. "You are a very dangerous person, Miss Merri."

"I am certain I told you that when we first met."

"Hmm." He pushed his thumb into the tender center of my foot and I melted back with a groan of pleasure. "That good?"

"Yes." I fell back into the bed.

He massaged my foot. "Shouldn't you be the least bit worried about spending the night with a man you just met?"

"Um… let me think. Should I be worried about the guy who offered me water to drink, told me when the clothes I was wearing might have been showing too much, and who suggested I sleep in the guest room instead of his bed?" I glared at him. "Yes. I should be terribly worried that he doesn't like me."

Seth raised an eyebrow. "I'm a Grim Reaper too, though. I've killed every relationship I've ever been in. The long-term thing? It's impossible."

I rolled on my side to look at him better, pulling my foot out of his grasp. "How many of those relationships did you kill?" He looked like he was ready to run, so I reached out and tugged at his shirt sleeve, pulling his unresisting body down to the bed with me.

We were eye to eye and I could see everything in the dark depths of his gaze.

The unspoken fears. The old pain. The last smoky wisp of dying hope…

"It wasn't you." I shook my head. "It wasn't ever you who killed the relationships, was it?"

Seth tucked his chin down, avoiding my gaze again. "I'm sure I had something to do with it. A handsome media mogul. I'm not the richest man in the world, but I'm not poor. But there was always something I did wrong. I worked too much. I was too quiet. I wasn't decisive enough. I didn't show them off enough." His shoulder lifted and fell in a shrug.

"Too loud. Too smart. Too mouthy," I recited the litany. "Too bright. Too colorful. Too feminine. There's always something that scares the weak ones away, isn't there?"

His smile finally returned, the first spring day after a long, cruel winter. "It's different with you. The light… follows you around. You walk into a room and it's like there was a party waiting to start. Me? I'm just that quiet kid writing horror movies and wearing a hoodie. I'm weird. I'm awkward. Who wants to spend a night sitting at home with me?"

"Oh! What a tragedy!" I put the back of my hand to my forehead like a silent movie actress in distress. "What is a person supposed to do with a night alone with you, Seth?" I fell back into the bed with a woeful look. "It only someone would hurry up and invent something for people to do as a couple at night, like watch movies, or talk. When will someone invent sex?"

Seth burst out laughing and rolled toward me. "Really?"

"Really." I nodded earnestly. "I just feel so bad for all those other people who met you and thought it was a burden to spend the night with you. They are going to die unloved and alone as virgins. It's such a tragedy." I touched his chest, picturing the ripped torso beneath his shirt as I licked my suddenly dry lips. "For them. Obviously. Not for me."

He was almost close enough to kiss, eyes caught on mine. "I take it you have plans."

"Mm hmm. Since your reputation as a player is already dead on arrival, I'm going to take the next available option: killing your bad habit of being single."

"Oh?" He tilted his head. "So I guess I get to kill your streak of not having a second date."

"I like the sound of that." Very, very much.

"Does tonight count as a first date?"

"I don't know, does it? Are we dating?" *Please say yes.*

I could feel the heat off Seth's lips but couldn't quite close the gap.

"We're dating." He pulled away.

I glared. "If we're dating where are you going?"

"Out of the room, because you haven't slept in two days." His smile was sly and challenging.

I pouted. "Stop thinking about my health and come flirt with me some more. This is fun."

"Tomorrow will be fun too."

I sat up. "Really?"

He grinned. "Once we get through our jobs, and the paperwork the police want you to fill out, and everything else, sure!"

"Ugh. Reality." I flopped back onto the bed. "That's no fun."

"What if we start with a breakfast date tomorrow?"

"Hmmm…" I made a show of considering the options. "I suppose that would help. But so would a kiss…"

Seth's smile was devastating and delicious. "If I kiss you goodnight, we're not going to get any sleep."

"Promise?"

"Promise. I'll prove it another night." He glided out the door, shutting it behind him.

Terrible, sexy, sensible man.

Why was it so easy to fall in love with the brainy ones? Who bothered to have practical thoughts about sleeping after being awake for fifty-one hours when there was someone as sexy as me available?

I fought a yawn and kicked at the bedspread.

Fine. I was tired. So what?

The pillow sank under my head as my eyes drifted shut. We could have at least cuddled. Seth had the perfect arms for cuddling.

He probably even snored cute.

It was a terrible, terrible thing to love an intelligent man.

I wondered what he thought about women proposing…

There's always something disconcerting about waking up in a strange bed, in a strange room. Especially when it's a strange guest room and the house is filled with the hollow sense of rejection.

Seth Morana, playboy of horror, had shot me down.

Ouch.

…On the bright side, he'd hinted at a real date, and he'd given me a spare charger for my phone so I could see the long list of messages and urgent requests from the police, asking me to come to the station at their earliest convenience.

I read that twice.

Yup.

Their earliest convenience, not mine.

How sweet.

It was after eight in the morning, so I called the dry cleaner who handled my dresses and talked to Chel.

We agreed the black dress with swallows was too aggressive and the red screamed *killer* a little too loudly, so we picked the deep, pine-green dress with pale pink cherry blossoms floating across it.[32]

Once She Of The Magic Cleaning Products texted to say a runner was on the way with my dress, I texted Dan at the police department to tell him I'd be there within the hour.

He told me to meet him at my apartment instead.

Ugh.

I knew they had to go in. This was a major security breach at a building that prided itself on the safety and anonymity they provided their tenants. Even if I didn't

---

[32] I realize that conversation gives off the impression that I have an unlimited dress supply hidden in the closet like some sort of magic superpower, but this isn't true. I have twenty-seven dresses total, and at any given time Chel has guardianship of eight of them for cleaning and repairs.

Dulcie Waterhouse might have been content with merely threatening payback, but plenty of other people thought throwing coffee, tea, wine, and—occasionally—trashcans at me was the way to go. Chel was the divine angel who made my dresses wearable again.

want more people in my house, the building owner would override it.

Or cancel my lease.

Double ugh.

Apartment shopping in spring was the worst.

Finger-combing my hair into soft, wide curls, I managed to smudge what remained of my evening makeup into something acceptable for day wear. I didn't look completely exhausted, just mildly wrung out.

A shame, really.

Exuberantly Tousled would have been a much better look for a night with Seth. Such was life.

I made my way to the kitchen, Killer tee hanging to my knees.

And found Seth, frozen, Final Boss mug in front of him and mouth hanging open. His loose, black pajama pants and soft, gray t-shirt looked very touchable.

I raised an eyebrow. "You okay?"

His gaze slowly swept down to my toes and back up. His perfectly delicious lips formed a silent word that looked like it started with f and rhymed with duck.

"Good morning."

"Good morning." Seth managed to get the words out without sounding completely stunned.

"Did you sleep well?" I opened the fridge and looked for anything quick and easy to grab. Sadly, none of the things in the fridge looked as fun as Seth.

I needed to get him out of my head. The man was a distraction.

Seth set his mug down with a thunk of finality. "We were both tired last night."

I turned around, eyes wide with innocence. "Did I say anything about that?"

"You—" Seth waved a hand up and down.

"I look good?" I guessed. Right. I shrugged. "I asked if you slept well. There wasn't any judgment."

"You were glaring," Seth said. "*Are* glaring. You're angry."

"I'm trying to find breakfast before my dress arrives. Once it's here, I have to go meet the police at my apartment, see what damage was done, and fill out a dozen forms. And all of that eats into time that should be spent sorting out Cozy's accounts."

Seth folded his arms across his chest. "So… that ice queen, destroyer-of-worlds look in your eyes isn't directed at me? At all?"

"Believe it or not," I said as I poured a glass of orange juice, "it's happened once or twice, where I had to pay the price of my beauty. Rejections happen."

"That wasn't a rejection. It was a flag on the play! You nearly died at the pool, spent all day acting like my fiancée, went to a gala to rescue Ellen and flirt with the mayor—"

"I was not flirting with the mayor!" I nearly choked on my orange juice. "His wife would kill me!"

"And then your apartment got broken into! It seemed like a high stress day!" Seth shook his head. "It didn't sound like a good day for impulsive, emotion-driven decisions."

"It was a day ending in y!" I put my juice next to his mint tea. "This is my life! It happens."

"Really? All the time?"

"Not the break-in," I admitted, "but the rest? Yes. Before I showed up at Slasher on Thursday, I'd already had one afternoon death threat and a green car tried to run me over. On Wednesday, I had four nasty emails and one doxxing attempt. Tuesday a former CFO who is headed to jail tried to kill me in the courtroom. On Monday…" I sorted through memories of Monday. "Monday, no one tried to murder me."

Poor Seth was staring at me with wide eyes and an open mouth—and an air of panic. I'd broken him.

"I'm the Grim Reaper of Chicago. Near death experiences are just part of the job."

Seth didn't look like he was going to survive this conversation.

"But I'd prefer near-Seth experiences." I fluttered my eyelashes and slipped into Seth's personal space. "If I'm not too scary for you."

Scary seemed to be the key to unlocking the horror-lover's heart. Seth's look of terrified confusion turned into a confident smirk. "Scary?" He reached out and pulled me to him. "Nothing scares me."

"Mmm?" I wrapped my arms around his neck. "You sure about that?"

"Nothing about *you* scares me." He dipped his head down for a good morning kiss. Finally!

Mint tea and orange juice… There was no way this combination was acceptable—unless I was kissing Seth.

I bit my lip as I pulled away. "Maybe I should switch to tea in the morning."

"Maybe." He was grinning.

My heart fluttered at the promise in his eyes.

The doorbell rang. Seth's eyes slitted as he glared at the intrusive sound.

"That's my dress, and my reminder that I have paperwork to do." I gave Seth another quick kiss before slipping out of his arms and tipping the delivery driver, who managed to get part of my name out before his eyes got stuck on my legs and he forgot how his tongue worked.

It was going to be one of those days.

I held the dress up for Seth to see. "What do you think?"

"I bet it will look fabulous on you."

I nodded. "Everything does."

"What's your schedule this week?"

"I don't know until I get a look at Oretega's books tomorrow. But..." I gave him a flirtatious smile. "I should be free for dinner tonight."

He smiled back. "I'd like that."

"What are you doing today?"

"Breakfast. Laundry. Then I need to go into the office and see if Alisson left the notes for the new script on her desk, because she didn't send them to me. I'll be there most the day, but I'll be home before dinner." With each word he came a little bit closer, sneaking up on me. "You can come back any time you want."

Standing on tiptoe, I gave him one last, regrettably quick kiss. "That's exactly what I wanted to hear."

Ninety-four minutes later, as another storm roared outside, I'd met with the police, confirmed my location with images from the art festival that were floating on the internet, and was staring at the absolute disaster of my closet. The white closet doors has been broken for no reason I could see other than that the intruder was angry. My dresses and petticoats lay strewn on the floor, smeared with tomato sauce from the pantry. My favorite green dress was torn.

Silk bras and lingerie had been ripped from the dresser drawers. The bed was in shambles, sheets torn off, the white lamp broken, the pillows on the ground. Even the white, Vienna matelassé curtains I'd had since I rented my first apartment were ripped. I was going to murder whoever broke into my apartment if the police didn't catch them first. I had connections. I could make a body disappear. Ellen would be my alibi.

Or Seth.

No, Ellen. She looked too cute and innocent to lie. The jury would like her better. Seth was sexy, and a better actor, but Ellen could cry on cue. That would work in my favor.

There was a polite cough behind me.

I turned away from the candy-colored carnage spread across the white carpets of my floor like a broken rainbow. "Yes, detective?"

Dan Kim wasn't as tall as Seth, or as young, but he had classical appeal. Dark eyes, dark hair, with a healthy tan from his genes and his habit of running near Lake Michigan every afternoon. Our paths crossed on a semi-regular basis, so I knew his story. Married his college sweetheart, lost her twelve years later to cancer, started dating again three years later, hated it, mostly permanently single but he wouldn't mind having a weekend brunch with me.

And now he was looking around my bedroom.

For the moment, plans for murder would have to wait. I smiled and let Detective Kim get an eyeful of my room. "Is it what you expected?"

"Not at all," he admitted. "Anything missing?"

I kicked at the fallen dresses. "Probably a few buttons. Nothing I can't get fixed."

"I didn't see any electronics."

"I have a laptop, nothing else. And that's in my car." Seth had taken me past the studios last night to collect the car, including my laptop and, more importantly at the time, my gym bag.

"Any jewelry?" Dan asked as he walked out of the bedroom. "Files? Anything at all?"

I followed, taking in everything I'd missed when I'd rushed to check on my dress collection.

All my drawers had been pulled out and slammed to the floor.

The one dish set I had was in the kitchen smashed to smithereens.

The couch had been flipped over and a plant knocked down, but... I shrugged. "Maybe they took some of the silverware? But it's the cheap stuff I had since college. It's worthless. There's damage, but I can't see anything missing. Maybe a kitchen knife? I haven't counted yet."

"Let the crime scene techs go over it." Dan motioned for me to exit. "We need to photograph this, just in case."

A cold chill settled over me. "Is that absolutely necessary? Even in the bedroom?"

"It won't be the first time your panties have been in the public domain," Dan joked.

I froze. Even if a trial didn't make those photos public domain—which it might—my past was well known enough to the Chicago PD that pictures would get passed around. People I had to work with on a daily basis would see my private place, my room, my clothes, my underwear, my bed... I absorbed the chill, let it soak into my bones and fill me so that when I met the detective's eyes, he withered and stepped back in fear.

"Sorry. Sorry. Bad joke."

"As a general rule, detective, it is considered poor form to harass the victim of sexual assault, even if it was a virtual assault. I was attacked when I was seventeen. It's not a joke to me. It never will be." I took a deep breath, shaking off the residual shame and anger. "Please leave."

"What?" Dan shook his head. "This is—"

"I'm not filing a report," I decided. "There was a noise complaint. I'll pay the fine, if there is one. But I'm not pressing charges. So you can leave."

"Merri, this is serious." Dan chased after me as I walked out. "I don't want the next crime scene I find to be one with your corpse!"

"And I don't want pictures of my lingerie shared with the police departments of seventeen counties." I didn't want to repeat the nightmare of my teen years. I didn't want to go to court and have the defending lawyer ask me if I was wearing a flirty Fleur du Mal thong under my A-line skirt. I didn't want everyone mentally undressing me.

Dan pressed his lips into a grimace. "Fine, how about a compromise? We won't take pictures of your private areas."

"My house is all a private area."

"Just the front door, kitchen, and living area," Dan said. "I'll give you a written apology if you want."

I smiled. It was a cold, dark, cruel smile that made his eyes widen in panic. "I do not want your apology. I want you out of my house. All of you. Now."

"Compromise, Merri!"

"A compromise would mean you were giving something to me, detective."

"Peace of mind?" he suggested.

I put my hands on my hips and sharpened my smile. "Really?"

The detective stomped, turned, swore, and turned back to me with a placating smile. "Let's try this again. I will...." He sighed. "Let's just sit down, go over the list of recent threats to your life, and go through a list of top ten most likely suspects. Just give me enough that—if you wind up dead—I have somewhere to start."

His pleas didn't move my heart.

"Sure," I said sweetly. "Let me offer you a place to sit and make you a snack but—oh!—wait. Right. I can't.

Perhaps we can reschedule and do this tomorrow at the office. I'll have the interns send you a list."

Storming out of my own apartment would have been nicely theatrical, but it wasn't really Dan I was angry at. I was angry at myself for not having this all figured out.

There is no such thing as Coincidence. That's simply the human brain trying to find the pattern between events. Sometimes there is one. Sometimes there isn't.

Today, there was definitely a pattern.

I could feel it, but I couldn't see it yet.

I blazed past the various police flunkies and went to the small, communal laundry room to sit in the gloom of the broken lights. A faulty wire needed replacing, but the super kept putting in new lightbulbs instead, so only the back wall was lit. A wall of silver washers on one side, a wall of black dryers on the other. The wobbly table between the two was black faux wood bracketed by two plastic chairs with twiggy legs.

Dan followed me in, shutting the door with its small, glazed window quietly. "Merri, I know you. What's up?"

"It's been a long week," I said, sitting with my back to the wall so I could see the door and window clearly. "Really, I just want my house back."

"Give me twenty more minutes," Dan said as he sat down across from me with a tablet and stylus out. "I'm serious, this is the kind of escalation that ends with tragedy. Give me a few minutes. Walk me through what's happened recently."

I shrugged. "I spent the week at Windy City Security looking into an embezzling case. It was fairly clear cut. Dulcie Waterhouse left Thursday afternoon. I got a call from the office saying a friend was looking for me." I stared past Dan to where the glow of his screen reflected off the tinted window of the laundry room.

"Friend?" Dan sounded suspicious.

"Ellen Berry from Cozy Studios. I've know her since grade school."

"Cozy does the romance movies, yes?"

"Yeah. They were bought by Slasher Studios in January and there was a hiccup in the accounting department when they merged. I went to do some pro bono work and help out."

Dan switched his screen to dark mode and white lines of script appeared on the window. "Any problems there?"

"None."

"No pushback from the Slasher CEO? What's his name? I saw him in the news."

"Seth Morana? He's a marshmallow."

Dan gauwffed at my word choice. "Horror's hottest actor is a marshmallow? Doubt it."

I let the comment pass. "Yesterday I went to Oretega Mineral Exchange to look at engagement rings—"

There was a snap and a ping.

I blinked. It took me a moment to realize Dan was holding half a stylus in his hand. He'd broken it.

"Engagement?"

"It was a scouting expedition," I said. "Oretega has hires Markham and Sloan to come in every five years for an audit. This is routine. Nothing important."

"Okay, but a fake engagement?" I could see Dan's screen change as he pulled up the public listing of company connections. My office used the same one, but only the public edition. His looked like the government edition. Dulcie's company had a lot more connections there. Interesting.

"It wasn't a fake engagement. It was ring shopping before the engagement," I said.

"Ah." Dan pretended to make a note but nothing new appeared in the reflection. "Has he picked a day to propose?"

"I'm getting him a custom ring, so I'll need to wait until it's done and then figure it out. I was thinking of waiting a month or two."

Maybe in October. The Halloween decorations would be up for the engagement photos. Or we could steal a set from Slasher.

My mind ticked over the possibilities as I watched Dan scroll morosely through his list of companies I was connected to.

Windy City Security and Anderson Financial and Darab Industrial and Slasher–Cozy and Oretega and…

Why was there a line between Windy City Security and Oretega? There was no reason for there to be a connection.

Unless Windy City Security installed the new systems for Oretega.

Details slotted into place.

The green car at Dulcie's office, the one that nearly ran me over the day I'd fired her, while she was holding a coffee cup from Heavenly Monday's and a bag of their macarons. The same macarons Yerke loved so much.

The car belonged to Yerke, the immoral jeweler.

Yerke had come to see me at Cozy.

Yerke knew Dulcie.

Someone had installed fake accounting software on the Cozy company computers. Someone with access to a company like Windy City Security.

I'd gotten Dulcie fired Thursday.

I'd talked to Yerke at Oretega Friday—after the incident with the green car, after the incident at the pool.

…And Yerke thought I was engaged to Seth.

Several very ugly words came to mind.

I guess even villains have grapevines.

"Merri?" Dan sounded concerned.

I pulled my phone out of my pocket and dialed Seth's number.

"Everything okay?"

"Sure." *Nope.*

"You need anything?"

"My purse and some water, if this is going to drag on."

Dan stood. "I'll go get that."

"Thanks."

Seth's phone went to voice mail.

I dialed again.

One of the rookies returned with my purse and mumbled something about Dan needing to take a call for a lieutenant that might take a while.

Seth's phone went to voice mail again.

I dialed Alisson.

Her phone was off.

My car was at Slasher studios, and there was a good chance Seth was too.

Which gave Yerke multiple targets.

I texted Dan from the elevator. He could meet me at the corner of Hooker and Weed.

The storm had shut down power to half the city and canceled all the outdoor filming for the day. I ran into a rain-soaked Nicah—three neon green stars matching his bright green, high-heeled boots—outside the main building as he waited for someone named Willa to come get him.

"Have you seen Seth?" I asked, taking as much shelter as I could under the eaves of the building.

Nicah nodded. "He's over on the big set prepping castle scenes for tomorrow."

Seth hadn't talked much about castles, sets, or any of the Slasher productions. "Where is that? Who's he with?"

"Nobody!" Nicah shouted over the rain as it grew heavier, the sound of it hitting the roofs and pavement almost defeaning. "Ianira sent everyone to get some sleep so we can shoot tonight!" A yellow sports car pulled into the gravel lot with a splash. "That's Willa. Got to go!" He took a half step and paused. "Seth should be over in the North Cherry building. Look for the zombie Santa!" He waved goodbye, sparkly black and purple bracelets flashing.

Zombie Santa. Right.

I tried Seth's phone again to no avail, and sighed. Was I being paranoid? Maybe.

But the incident at the pool hadn't been an accident. The attack on my apartment looked angry.

I tried Dan's phone, but all I got was a busy signal that shunted me to voicemail. I left a quick message in case he checked that before reading my text, then tucked the phone into my pocket.

I needed to know Seth was safe, that I hadn't killed my first chance at happiness by dragging him into the messy world of Merri Kriesmas.

Running through the pelting rain, I crossed the Cozy backlot full of cheerful small towns filled with ghosts of movies past and into the large sets of Slasher's *Holiday Of Horrors*. As if Santa Claus wasn't sinister enough—knowing when you were sleeping, knowing when you weren't—Slasher had taken the idea of the enslaved elven population of the North Pole and turned them into flesh-eating zombies wearing candy-striped rompers.

I know horror is social commentary about the fears and anxieties of the majority populace played out in a monstrous, allegorical way.[33] The Christmas elves were

---

[33] I said Seth didn't talk about his projects much with me. I didn't say I didn't do my own research or shamelessly eavesdrop while wandering a movie studio for the past few days.

undoubtedly representative of the down-trodden workers abused by an all-controlling, all-seeing, judgmental demigod figure, with the presents representing the distractions of mass entertainment—which made the whole 'mass entertainment is a disease' message a little ham-handed—but stopping in the workshop of death with a life-sized model of the actors sprawled across a reflective pool of fake blood was still a little unnerving.

Especially Mrs. Claus in her twee red-and-white A-line and apron, with her head fractured because of a fall.

I paused to take a breath and looked into the gloom as lightning split the sky.

The building was huge, home to the interior sets for at least three movies, plus the storage for other sets and workrooms for the props department. It had all been explained in the budget sheets Alisson had showed me, but seeing it was something else.

It was endless darkness, lit only by multi-colored ever-glow holiday lights running off solar panels, and what little light snuck through the skylights high overhead.

"Seth?" Every sound was swallowed up, erased almost as soon as I heard it. My blood drummed in my ears as my breathing echoed the dripping of my clothes on the warehouse floor. There were baffles... Baffles? Was that the word? It sounded like the word. Pieces of soundproof material dividing the stages, because Slasher relied on on-set recordings, while Cozy favored dubbing.

Right.

I could do facts.

Facts were good.

So was finding Seth.

The set wasn't perfectly soundproof, not with the wide, rolling walls pushed aside so sets could be moved between stages. I closed my eyes, trying to focus like I did in yoga class since seventh grade: listen and forget.

One by one I eliminated sounds: the rain drumming on the roof, the heaving sigh of the overworked air conditioning, the creaks and groans of the walls battered by the wind, until all that was left was a hushed, scrabbling sound like sandpaper brushing across starched fabric. I ran after that sound.

Lightning illuminated a path through the wonderland of Slasher nightmares. Twice I slowed for a prop corpse, only to dash on again looking for Seth.

There was an inarticulate shout and a thump up ahead.

And a wall.

The wooden wall of the church set for Ellen's follow–your–heart holiday movie, currently being borrowed for a jilted–at–the–altar lover scene by Slasher, stretched from the anchor wall of the building to the door. I tried the stained-glass door first. It was locked.

When the lightning flashed again, on the other side of the stained glass I could see Yerke standing behind Seth.

Seth slumped to the floor, lips blue.

I banged at the door, unheard over the rain.

Where were the police? Dan should be here by now. This wasn't complicated.

Fighting the locked door was no good, and Ellen would kill me if I ruined the stained glass. I ran back to the fake church wall, pushing with one hand at the reinforced Styrofoam as the other fumbled for my blue clutch. Wallet, phone, perfume, lip gloss—and wool socks I kept for days when the office was chill. My eyes fell on a pile of rubble. I nudged one of the fist-sized rocks with my foot and felt actual stone. Good. Socks and rocks. Not a perfect weapon, but mass and velocity would be on my side.

I found a weak point on the wall, pushed my through, and found myself boxed in on three sides, watching helplessly through another fake stained glass window as Seth struggled to breath in front of an old-fashioned street lamp on a small-town street dusted with fake snow.

Seth kicked his feet, one hand tugging at whatever Yerke had wrapped around his throat, and the other trying to push off the ground.

How the ever lovin' eff was I supposed to get out of this box? Running through the studio was like jumping between parallel universes and always landing one thin veil of reality away from where I wanted to be.

"Seth! Yerke!" I pounded my fist on the wood of the window frame. If nothing else I could let Yerke know there was a witness. Maybe he'd back off.

Maybe he didn't hear me at all.

Along the set of the small-town street, the soft glow of the lanterns illuminated a nightmare. Seth's lips were turning dark. He was dying and I was trapped, watching.

Seth twisted, grabbing Yerke's arm.

Yerke jerked as if shocked. The older man's face went slack.

Seth's face looked like a skull, sunken cheeks and dark eyes unnaturally wide. He held Yerke as the older man slumped slowly to the ground. In the next flash of lightning, Seth looked skeletal. And furious.

His grasp on Yerke tightened, then he pulled his hand away as if burned. Clutching at his neck, Seth stumbled forward, crashing against the wooden wall between us.

The wall between us withered. Aging and cracking under Seth's touch. The glass fell with a crash and spun in place before falling over in the otherwise silent room.[34]

Color returned to Seth's face as the wood rotted, leaving nothing but air between us. His eyes widened with fear and pain. "Merri?"

Outside, the howling wind died.

The rain stopped.

All that was left was me and Seth, standing in the middle of a winter fantasy with a dying man sprawled in front of Santa's throne.

Seth shrank in on himself. "Merri."

I raised my eyebrows.

"You—you said you were a Grim Reaper." Seth was

---

[34] Turns out on-set accidents are common enough that they use safety glass. I wouldn't have been able to break it if I'd tried.

inching away from me. "You're... you're not this kind of Reaper, are you?"

"No." I drew the word out, swinging the rocks in my sock from side to side as I reviewed the facts. "Did you kill Yerke?"

"No." Seth shook his head quickly. "No. No. I wouldn't. I didn't want to hurt him. It was instinct. I swear on my life, Merri, I'd never hurt you."

"I know that. What did you do to him?"

Yerke was pale and still on the floor. Not corpse-like, but like he'd caught the worst bout of flu in his life and ran a marathon before collapsing.

"Just... borrowed," Seth said.

"So, I did see you drain the life out of him?" I asked for clarification. "You sucked out his life to stop him and then—" I looked down at where the wall had been. "You killed the set?"

Seth's hand moved from his neck to his chest, rubbing over his heart. "I need death to survive. A human life is easy to take. But I can take something else. The set... The set can be replaced. Yerke can't."

The world would move along perfectly well without Yerke, but Seth looked guilty enough as it was that I didn't want to complicate things. "What will happen to him?"

"He'll die a few years sooner than he would have if he hadn't met me," Seth said in a small voice.

I sniffed. "It's still decades longer than he would have lived if I'd gotten to him first," I said as I put my sock and rocks away, testing the limits of my clutch's capacity. "Is there duct tape anywhere?"

Seth's eyebrows collided in confusion. "What?"

"Duct. Tape." I enunciated it better the second time. "The police are coming and Yerke could cause a lot of trouble if he ran off."

"Merri, I—"

I patted Seth's arm and walked past him to the lighting setup. Camera people had duct tape, didn't they? Or string?

Even the cords would do in a pinch.

But there was duct tape. Good, old reliable fix for all things Midwestern. Duct tape could repair roofs, be turned into prom dresses, and hold would-be murderers until the cops showed up.

Yerke's eyes opened in an unfocused stare as I taped his wrists together. The police were not going to believe he'd simply stopped.

Frowning, I dug into my purse again and found my rose-petal perfume, a barely-there floral fragrance that doubled as an assault weapon.[35]

"What are you doing?" Seth asked as I shook the bottle.

"Establishing an alibi." I sprayed the perfume directly into Yerke's face a couple of times.

The scent of roses and the bond jeweler's shrieks of pain filled the air.

I nodded as I heard police sirens in the distance. "There. Yerke tried to choke you. I ran in and sprayed my perfume in his eyes. The pain made him step back,

---

[35] Also? An accelerant. Because you never know when you'll need a tiny Molotov cocktail.

which is when he tripped and hit his head. Aside from a mild concussion, and the irritants in his eyes, he's fine. Self-defense. Case closed." I put my perfume away.

Seth was shivering.

I stepped toward him.

He stepped away.

"Seth—"

"I'm sorry," he blurted out. "I'm sorry. I thought you were—" He shook his head, looking at the ground. "I'm sorry. I wouldn't hurt you, or anyone. It was instinct."

"You said that already."

He took a shuddering breath, face thinning, his high cheekbones becoming more and more pronounced. For a moment his face was almost skeletal again.

I raised an eyebrow. "Cute trick." I winked at Seth. He could think he was scary all he wanted, but I'd already made up my mind: Seth Morana was mine. And I never, ever, lost what I wanted.

There was the sound of running feet. "Merri?"

"Dan!" I shouted and waved into the darkness. Ugh. Useless. I took out my phone and turned the light on. "I'm right here!"

Seth stepped away from me as the police ran up, his cheeks plumping up as some of the fake snow fizzled into ash at his feet with an acrid scent.

Dan slowed as he approached, looked at me, then Seth, then down at Yerke. "What happened?"

"I left you a message," I said, not even trying to keep the exasperation out of my voice. "Yerke was targeting Mister Morana. I came here to warn him because his phone was off."

"It's in my office," Seth said quietly. "But probably on."

I waved away that detail. "I came to warn him and found Yerke choking Mister Morana."

One of the police officers who had run in after Dan shone a flashlight on Seth.

There was an ugly red line around his neck that was going to be a hideous bruise in a few days.

Another officer stooped over Yerke and hauled him to his feet.

"Then what happened?" Dan asked. "Why'd Yerke stop?"

"Perfume," I said. "I had some in my purse." I dug in my purse and pulled it out again. "It's non-toxic and supposedly hypoallergenic, but it stings if it hits your eyes. I'm really very sorry if Mister Yerke has permanent damage." No I wasn't. "I didn't know what else to do."

Dan took the perfume bottle, sniffing at it as if it could be anything else. The smell of roses filled the air again.

Yerke yelped and tried to shake the police officer off. "That's not what happened!"

One of the police pulled out a notepad. "What happened?"

"He tried to kill me!" Yerke screamed as he shook his taped together hands at Seth. "His face turned into a skeleton and he tried to kill me. I was dying!"

"Riiiggghhht." Dan made the universal facial expression that meant Someone Is Not Addressing Reality Today.

"I saw it!" Yerke yelled. "She saw it! He took down the whole wall. Made it crumble! He's Death! He's Death!"

"And his eyes glowed red?" I said in a tone of chilly scorn. "I've seen that movie too, Yerke. But this is a movie *set*, not an actual movie."

Dan made a note of that too. "Red eyes?"

"*Unforgiven?*" I asked. "Have you seen the movie?"

"Oh, yeah, I loved that movie in college!" Dan looked over at Seth. "That was you?"

Seth nodded reluctantly.

"She's lying! Ask about the wall!" Yerke shouted. "Ask about the wall! Where's the wall?"

To his credit, Dan looked skeptical. There was obviously a piece of the set missing. "You saw everything?" he asked again.

I nodded as I smiled. "Yes. Everything."

"And he"—the detective pointed at Seth —"didn't turn into a soul-sucking skeleton."

"Oh, he did," I said as my smile grew warmer. "Seth turned into a skeleton and sucked several years off Yerke's life to keep himself alive. And I'm a tooth fairy. I have a castle in the clouds. Huge, huge castle. Ginormous. Made of teeth. And I have these little tiny wings that are invisible and I have a wand." I rolled my eyes. "While we're at it, is this a good time to confessing to being the Loch Ness Monster too?"

The police all chuckled.

"Right," Dan said. "Silly question."

"Exceptionally so," I said.

Yerke jerked away from the officer holding his arm. "He made a wall dissolve! It's gone! Look at the floor!"

The police all looked at the floor.

I sighed. "What Mister Yerke saw was a special effect that—" I stopped talking and covered my mouth with my hand. "Oh! That, that isn't public information is it?" I turned to Seth.

Seth stared at me in silent bewilderment.

"You said the technique for aging the sets was unique to Slasher," I said, hand feeding him the story. "Detective Kim, what Yerke saw was a special effect. And I think he probably needs to sign an NDA."

That got Seth back to the real world. "A non-disclosure agreement?" he asked. "Do you think that's necessary?"

"Yerke saw it," I said, "and the police will hear about it during the course of the investigation. I'm not your lawyer, but I do advise you to have everyone sign an NDA before they leave. Obviously this may come out in court, but you should at least try to protect your special effects. Alisson was telling me just the other day about how this one was poised to win you awards."

Seth blinked, but to his credit he didn't argue. He looked at the detective and then at Yerke. "I guess?"

"Great!" I clapped my hands together with a cheerful smile. "I'll go to the office to help Mister Morana print the NDAs and then you can take our statements. Will that work?"

Detective Kim nodded. "Sure. Can we have the security footage too?"

Over Yerke's dead and cooling corpse.

"I'm sure no one objects." I nodded at Seth. "The power wouldn't have turned them off, would they?"

"The security cameras might have been running," Seth allowed, each word moving with the slow force of an ancient grudge. "But I don't know. We can check."

"We'll need that and statements from both of you," Detective Kim said. "EMS would like to check you out Mr. Morana. And, Merri" —he hit me with what he probably considered a killer smile—"my personal number is on the back. Call me if you need anything."

I took his card with a warm smile. "Of course, Dan. You know I will." Over my dead and cooling body.

I kept my smile in place until the police filed out and then tossed Dan's card in a small bin in the corner between sets. Yerke was out of the picture. The only problem that remained was the horrified look on Seth's face, and the shame in his eyes when he looked at me.

Good thing I'd never yet met a problem I couldn't solve.

Thanks to the theatrics of my spontaneous three-day weekend, the Oretega accounts were done in a trice. I'm not sure I would have spotted all the irregularities—or connections to Windy City Security—if Yerke hadn't panicked and tried to kill anyone.

There's a lesson there. If you're going to do crime, don't panic. Fear is a poor substitute for logic.

So is lust.

Logic couldn't explain why the coffee table in my living room was spread with background checks on everyone from Slasher–Cozy Studios, or why there was an unopened box of condoms by my bed and a still-sealed pack of mint tea in my cupboard.

Seth hadn't called. No one from Slasher–Cozy Studios had called.

I was in a wasteland of radio silence and growing more impatient by the minute.

So. Better to try and fail than never try at all. Right?

The plan was simple. I was going to steal one more thing from Seth Morana's office: Him.

Step one, remove the guard dog.

Simple enough. Lucky had a three-day weekend coming up, a motorcycle, and a look that could get her practically anyone she wanted. Alisson wouldn't stand a chance.

Step two, remove the clutter.

The Cozy side wasn't a problem, Ellen only had Patrick Miles for another twenty-four hours and I'd arranged a tour of Chicago. With those two gone, there was no reason for Seth to do anything.

But clearing the neon goths out of the Slasher building was going to take some cheating.

An extra ace up my sleeve as it were.

On my laptop, I pulled up the website for Extra Aces, the one-time theater group–turned–bar warmers who made a living by making sure any party in town was warm, inviting, and flirtatious. All of them were extroverts, several were asexual, two were named Ace legally, and if I told them I need a flock of goths kept busy at a bar near Slasher, they'd do it at a discount because they liked me.

Weird, I know. Someone liked me.

I cut that thought off. Lots of people liked me. Willow thought I was a great boss. Lucky said I was a great big sister. Ellen said I was a good friend.

Plenty of people liked me.

I need to focus on the heist.

What was the appropriate outfit for breaking into a person's workplace, killing their bachelorhood, and stealing their heart? Maybe something floral?

The poster of *Unforgiven* stared at me from my computer screen, Seth's dark eyes piercing into my soul. The last time I'd seen him, he'd been going into shock as he was bundled away by the police, who had all sorts of questions.

There were plenty of reasons for him not to call me. Shooting schedules. Script rewrites. Casting decisions.

Yesterday, I'd gone as far as to make an account on Everil so I could follow Seth's all-in-one social feed. The last picture he posted was of me standing in front of his window looking out at the storm and the caption, 'Perfect.'

So perfect he'd dropped off the face of the Earth and hadn't returned a single phone call. Okay, granted, his number had been auto-redirected to my office while I was deep in Oretega's numbers, and my phone had been off while I was at the courthouse earlier testifying on a different case, but still. Willow would have left me a message if Seth called.

And now his number was set to come directly to my phone. Which was sitting on the glass tabletop. Silent. Zero messages.

All my calls went directly to his voice mail.

Drumming my fingers next to a picture of Lucky in black leather riding gear, I wondered if this was worth it. Maybe this was Seth's not-so-subtle sign that he wasn't interested in anything more. I mean, sure, he'd kissed me and made my world spin, and he'd looked at me like I was the only person who mattered, but actors were a temperamental lot. I was his sun, moon, and stars—for a minute. And now the minute was over, and he'd fallen out of love.

It would be embarrassing if I went over and he didn't want me.

It'd be humiliating.

...It'd be better than sitting here wondering.

There was a knock at the door.

I glared at the newly installed, freshly painted portal of glossy black and tried to imagine who would knock at my door at eight o'clock on a Wednesday night. Lucky had a JV volleyball game. My parents were lecturing about the seventeenth century and weren't using cars or phones this week again. That left... Who?

A neighbor maybe?

The knock came again.

Frowning, I stood and crossed the small living room, walking past the tiny galley kitchen and equally tiny dining space to the teeniest foyer in Chicago, and hit the camera.

Seth was standing outside, holding a set of bags. He knocked again, glancing over his shoulder to see if he was disturbing anyone.

With a polite smile in place, I opened the door. The smell of his sandalwood soap hit me first, tugging at something primal that made me want to wrap my arms around him.

The look in his eyes was wary, like a beaten puppy at the adoption center hoping against hope that this time would be better.

"I think I've seen this movie. *Death Comes Knocking*."

Seth didn't laugh.

"Are you coming in?" I asked, forcing myself to step back so he had room.

"Do you mind?" His voice was quiet, apologetic. "Are you in the middle of something?"

"Just planning a heist."

Seth's eyes narrowed as he stepped inside and slid off his shoes. "A heist?"

I nodded. "There's something I wanted to steal."

Turning, I sashayed away in front of him, fully aware of the effect I had at home. White walls. Polished black wood floors. Black countertops and chairs. A sofa so white it almost split into distinct colors and an equally white, soft rug under the coffee table of black wood and glass. The pictures on the walls were monochrome prints of famous pictures known for their colors.

In my entire apartment, the only pop of color was my Mediterranean-blue dress—splashed with bright pink hibiscus—and the pink silk hibiscus tucked into my red curls.

Seth couldn't take his eyes off me.

Which was fair, because after not seeing anything but his movie posters for three days, all I wanted to do was stare back. His platinum hair was slightly messy, like he'd been running his hands through it while waiting for me to answer. His usual black hoodie had been replaced by a sexy black button down, black slacks instead of jeans.

"Were you going somewhere dressy tonight?" I asked.

Seth looked down at his clothes, licking his lips and frowning. "Um. No. No, just to see you."

"That isn't your usual work attire." I circled the coffee table, keeping some distance and trying to figure out why he was here. "Is everything all right?"

"I don't know." He pressed his lips together. "I... I brought dinner." He held up pale cloth bags with the logo of a nearby locavore market. "Bread and cheese. Salad. Fruit. Picnic stuff."

That didn't clarify anything. "How'd you get my address?"

"Alisson called Lucky."

My shoulders relaxed. "Really?"

Seth nodded. "They're meeting for dinner to-morrow."

Ha! I knew it. "You realize you're going to lose Alisson until Monday, right? Lucky has a three-day week-end." Was it too early to pick an outfit for the wedding? Probably. I could see Lucky wanting a spring wedding. Something mid-March-ish.

"What are you plotting?" Seth asked.

"Wedding clothes." I blinked and then realized he was kneeling by the coffee table, salads forgotten as he looked through my notes.

A small grin tugged at the corner of his lips. "What were you planning to steal, Miss Merri?"

I smiled back at him. "You."

He picked up the picture of Lucky next to her bike. I was there too, in black jeans and a black leather jacket with three grinning skulls that had gems in their eyes. People rarely got close enough to see, but the gems all had the number twenty embroidered on them. Over the skulls were the words TRIPLE KILL, our riding club, stitched in metallic pink thread.

A slightly smaller line of text underneath read PER-FECT SCORE, my nickname when I bothered to use it.

"You look good in black."

"So I've been told."

Seth put the picture back on the table and sat on the floor.

After a moment's hesitation, I sat down too. "So."

"So." He folded his hands in his lap and didn't look at me.

"Did you come here to talk?"

"I don't know." Seth sighed, unfolded a little, ran a hand through his hair, and hit me with a hungry look that made me want to crawl over and kiss him until he smiled again. "I don't know where to start. What to explain. I thought you were like me."

"And... I'm not?"

"You said you were a Reaper, so I thought you were. A real one. Like me." He took a deep breath, eyes fixed on the edge of the table. "I need death to survive."

"Everything does."

"Yeah, but most people can get nutrients from eating dead plants or dead animals. I need the *emotions* of death. The grief. The loss. The fear." He folded his arms. "It's a biological thing. In our early teens, we stop getting enough nutrients from regular food. We starve, or we find a way to feed on death. We work as butchers, exterminators, or in the medical field. My mom was an ER surgeon for years until they forced her to retire early. Then she died. Fast."

I scooted a little closer.

Seth curled in on himself even more. "She was used to the pain and trauma of the ER. The fear and death. Without it, she withered. Wasted away in only a few months. Her liver and kidneys shut down. No amount of food could feed her, and we didn't have a diagnosis that would get her into a nursing home. She wasn't quite sixty."

"I'm sorry."

A weak smile crossed his face. "My dad survived on aging things, stealing the life of objects. He taught me. But, plastics and all the new stuff isn't really filling. Horror films… Horror films worked. It's the same emotions and fears in the audience. The deaths feel real. It's like eating a tofu burger when you want a steak, but it gets the job done."

"All right." I nodded. "So you're a vegan Reaper?"

Finally he looked up at me. "I thought… When you said you were the Grim Reaper of Chicago, I thought you were like me. I thought it was safe to be in love with you."

"It is."

Seth shook his head. "I could hurt you."

"So could anyone."

"Merri—"

I put my hand on his knee. "Humans are predators. All of us. Anyone you meet has the ability to kill you. And our bodies have serious design flaws. We can die during childbirth. Do you know how many other mammals have the maternal mortality rates our species does? Not many. Honestly, I don't think any other mammal has the same incident rate. Pregnancy doesn't regularly kill elephants. But that's a risk that happens."

Seth's eyes were wide with terror.

Probably not a very convincing speech. "Sorry, my parents are historians. I grew up hearing all the ways human bodies could fail. All the creative ways humans can hurt each other. Your need for a chaser of horror movies after dinner is really not an issue."

"You saw me—"

"I saw you defend yourself from someone who tried to kill me three times."

Seth went rigid as his eyes went wide. "Three?"

"I did the math," I said with a shrug. "He tried to hit me with his car after I fired Dulcie Waterhouse. Windy City Security did computer work for Oretega and Dulcie was on the take. So Yerke was already running scared. Then he came to the gym. It *was* baby oil, he spilled it on purpose hoping I'd fall, crack my head, and at least be off the job, if not dead. And then he broke into my apartment with plans to hurt me. When he couldn't get me, he went after you."

With a quick glance, Seth assured himself I was unharmed. "You seem calm."

"Death threats are part of my job description."

"You're an accountant," Seth said in exasperation.

I shrugged and patted his knee. "Math is scary."

Closing his eyes, Seth leaned his head back on the couch. "This conversation is off script."

"What were you expecting?" I didn't bother hiding my amusement.

"I don't know. I had this whole noble speech about how you'd be safer with someone else, and this idea of seeing you again in a year, happy and married to some normal person."

It took effort, but I managed to turn my laugh into a choked cough as my cheeks turned red.

Dark eyes slitted open to glare at me. "It was very heroic."

"I'm sure it was," I said soothingly. "Any normal girl would have fallen for it, too. The curse of a forbidden romance. Long, hungry looks across some public venue. The sound of your heart breaking as you read the wedding announcement in some gossip column online. I'm sure you had the whole tragedy staged in your mind."

He shifted, curiosity overtaking his features. "Can you really see yourself taking a Reaper home for the holidays?"

I leaned closer, giving Seth an excellent view of my ample assets straining at the buttons of my bodice. "My parents are currently dressed as seventeenth-century pirates and lecturing on the medicine of the era. It's bloody. It's gruesome. If you went, you'd probably gain ten pounds from the dinners alone. Nothing you can say will shock my family."

To his credit, I think Seth got most of that. His eyes only dipped to my cleavage a couple of times. His pupils had widened in appreciation and the pulse in his neck had sped up a little, but that could have been fear of a family dinner. A totally normal reaction to the threat of a Kriesmas holiday.

"You said you brought dinner?" Standing up, I smoothed my skirt down, almost sad I hadn't worn something interesting underneath to lift the hem a little.

"Yeah." Seth's gaze caressed my legs, glided up my body, and met mine with a confident smirk.

I raised an eyebrow in challenge. If he wanted to have a sexy staring contest, I was more than willing to play. "Hungry?"

"Not for salad."

It turns out, I was wearing the perfect outfit to steal Seth's heart, the one with the missing top button…

Seth smiled as he kissed me, conquering me, seducing me, taking over my world so completely that my only thoughts were of him.

The only thing I craved was his skin against mine.

The only thing I wanted was his whispered confessions of love.

The only thing I needed was him beside me, always.

All the wants I'd pushed away, all the emotions I'd locked under my armor, all the secret desires I'd kept hidden were out now. Seth had stolen them from me with whispers and kisses. He'd destroyed every fear with soft words and softer touches.

There was no going back from this.

I'd built walls around myself once, cut myself off from every kind of love and relationship as I tried to protect myself. But I couldn't do it again.

Seth nuzzled my hair. "I can hear you thinking. What's wrong?"

I wanted to lie and say it was nothing. Or distract him with a kiss. But I couldn't bring myself to smile and lie.

"Merri," Seth whispered in my ear. "Why aren't you happy?"

"I am." I caressed his arm, trying to memorize the feel of his touch, the weight of his body against mine. "I'm afraid I'll lose you."

He kissed my cheek, my nose, my lips, feather-light touches that made me feel like I was glowing. "You won't lose me. I'm hard to miss."

I laughed despite my fears. "I'm very easy to miss. And not very loveable."

Seth kissed me again, drinking me in. "You're perfect. Exquisite. Unforgettable. Unsurpassable." He pulled me closer. "Addicting, possibly. And so, so easy to love. I've known you a week and already you're all I think about. I held up a decision about a location shoot because it would take me out of town for a few weeks and I wanted to check with you first. Sunday night I scribbled out a rough draft of a horror movie with a redhead and I might have to give it to Ellen because it has way more kissing than Slasher's movies do.

"I want to synch calendars with you, which sounds like the most unromantic thing a man could say, but I want to. I want to know when I can see you again. When I can kiss you again. When I can hear your voice." He stroked my cheek. "I wanted to talk to you all week."

"Why didn't you call?"

"My phone…" Seth ran a hand through his hair and looked embarrassed. "Um, so, I did take it with me when I went to the warehouse. And I dropped it—"

"Outside in the rain?"

"In the rain," he confirmed with a nod. "It's been in rice for days, but I think I'm going to have to give up and get a new one."

"I thought you were avoiding me. And then I had the Oretega accounts, and a trial, and…" So many other things.

"We both have busy lives," he said. "That's not going to change."

"I've never tried to fit a relationship into my work schedule."

"Neither have I," Seth said as his hand found mine, "but we're smart. We can make it work."

I pressed my lips together as tears threatened to fall. "Really?"

"You stole my shirt. You stole my time. You stole my heart." Seth's hungry gaze met mine. "What do you think about killing our reps as perpetually single people and making this official?"

Taking a deep breath, I squinted my eyes in mock suspicion. "I dunno, are you really ready to tangle with the Grim Reaper of Chicago? Are you okay with a girlfriend who gets death threats every week? I'm cute, but I'm not nice. I like math, and I can't sit still through movies, and I—I—"

"You're perfect." Seth kissed me again and I forgot all my excuses.

SIX MONTHS LATER: MID-OCTOBER

A strong gust of wind blew across the balcony, bringing a flurry of orange leaves that railed against the glass like souls begging for *entrée*. The Windy City was once again living up to its name. I hung our Halloween costumes on the door to the guest bedroom. A tight, black dress with ruby-red embellishments for my Hades costume, and gray-and-lilac harem pants and crop top with ribbons for Seth's Persephone. The silk flower crown was already sitting on his dresser.

Seth made a very menacing Persephone.

My case work for the day was sitting on the low table in the living room, a mess of math and printed copies of the relevant company rules that had been broken. Maple View Pharmaceuticals was getting a new CFO.

An autumn storm grumbled over the lake front as I changed from the bright yellow A-line with red hibiscus flowers to a pair of loose, black lounge pants and a Slasher t-shirt that fell off my shoulders. I traded my Victory Rolls for a sloppy bun and wiped off the last of my fire-red lipstick.

The woman who stared back in the mirror, the one without the candy-colored armor, looked dangerous. The broken, ignored little girl was gone. The fake girl from the videos was nowhere to be seen. I'd used my armor as a cocoon and had emerged, transformed into something new.

"Merri?" Seth's voice came from the front entry-way.

"In here." I walked out of the bedroom to see Seth juggling two bags of groceries and a slim DVD case in his hand with a suspiciously cheesy fake cover. "Is that what I think it is?"

"Dinner and the final cut of the Cozy Christmas special."

I took a bag from him and the case. "Why do you have a copy?"

"Because you and Ellen both yelled at me for not watching Cozy's movies?" He hung his keys on the hook by the fridge and put the food on the counter. "Want to watch?"

"Sure."

An hour later, we were sprawled out across the living room, me laying on the couch with my feet kicking the air, Seth sitting beside the couch chatting as he took notes.

On screen, Laurie Moore stood in paint-splattered jeans and t-shirt, making a wish on a shooting star as it broke into three pieces. A new image came up with the words, 'Who do you choose?'

Seth grinned up at me. "Ready for this?"

"Hmmm... almost." I kicked forward so I could drape my hands over his shoulders. "It's hard to pick a favorite."

"All you have to do is pick the hero she gets a happily ever after with for the rest of her life."

"Uh-huh." I reached past Seth to the small black box I'd hidden under the couch days ago.

Seth touched my other hand. "Who do you want to spend the rest of your life with?"

"You?" I flipped the box lid up, revealing the silver wedding band with intricate obsidian scrollwork we'd seen at Oretega back in April.

I'm fairly certain Seth stopped breathing.

I kissed his cheek. "What do you think? A lifetime of Kriesmas dinners, two sisters-in-law for the price of one, and I never have to say Merry Christmas outside of December for the rest of my life."

Seth's eyes went wider.

"Will you marry me?"

He clicked the TV remote and the screen changed to show Seth, larger than life, smiling at us.

On screen he got down on one knee. "Merri Kriesmas, you stole my time, my soul, and my heart. I'd like to give you my last name. Will you marry me?"

The real Seth sat tight-lipped, staring straight ahead like he'd seen the ruin of all things.

I hugged his shoulders. "Are you mad I beat you to asking, or happy that I asked, or anxious because you aren't sure what to do next?"

"Yes."

"Yes to which question?"

"Yes to all of them."

I giggled and slipped the ring on his left hand. "I love you."

"Merri Kriesmas, I love you too.[36]"

---

[36] Yeah, I know. Now I'm Meredith Morana, Merri Death. Mare-o'-death Death. Seth is already working on a script called *Night Mares* about horses of death. He is *so* weird. And I love him. The end.

ACKNOWLEDGMENTS

As always, there are people I need to thank for getting this book finished and into your hands.

To my ever-patient husband, thank you for "talking about my books with me" even though we both know you are going to sit there, smiling quietly while I ramble for an hour. You have solved many a plot problem by simply being there. I love you.

To my dear children who have to deal with the fact that mommy's brain might be in the wrong galaxy, and who are frequently consulted on what dresses my characters should wear, thank you for your patience, advice, and your willingness to suggest everything from gruesome murder ideas to facts about mythology.

To my beta readers, crit partners, and friends... I tried to keep it short!!!

As always, thank you to my readers from all over the globe and internet, including my Patreon crew: Amy Johnson, Glinda Harrison, Jackie Bach, John Morgan, Morgan Kegan, Tímea Knoll, Gwen Iacona, Clare Williams, Tonya Cannariato, and Bishop O'Connell.

Special thanks to Bishop O'Connell, fellow author and wordsmith, who graciously allowed me to use him as a character in this series. Bishop's fans will recognize a few names in the Oretega scene. If you'd like to learn more about Bishop and his books you can find him on the web at https://aquietpint.com/ and on Twitter at @BishopMOConnell.

Thank you, dear reader, for reading this book.

Love,
Liana

ABOUT THE AUTHOR

LIANA BROOKS loves spending her winter holidays surrounded by white sandy beaches, good books, and good company. She currently lives in South Carolina where the beaches are open all year, and fondly remembers her younger years when she went to Miami to read *The Odyssey* on South Beach.

She loves beaches, but never really learned how to party.

When not surrounded by books, Liana spends her time hiking, playing near the river, and keeping up with her busy family.

Liana is known for her space operas, including the *Fleet of Malik,* a series of connected sci-fi romances about rebuilding after a decades long war; the enemies-to-lovers superhero series, *Heroes and Villains*; and the *Time and Shadows* time travel murder mysteries.

You can find out more about Liana at her website, www.lianabrooks.com.

ALL I WANT FOR CHRISTMAS IS A WEREWOLF

THERE WAS MISTLETOE OVER MY DESK. HONEST TO goodness mistletoe hanging over the remains of my Halloween festivities. The Great Pumpkin was now overshadowed by a hemiparasitic shrub.

When I'd left for a conference two hours ago, my desk had been a bastion against the winter holidays. A snow-free island in an otherwise elegantly decorated office suite dedicated to art.

The gallery's front foyer with the dark wood paneling and over-stuffed pine-green tub chairs was now displaying glass-and-metal snowflakes in dazzling designs.

The main negotiating room, with the long table suitable for a fleet of lawyers, had a festive Seasons Greetings banner with pine trees and bright red birds signed by various Miami athletes.

The hall had garlands, multi-colored lights, and occasionally holiday music blaring out of incautiously opened offices.

But this?

This monstrous greenery was not supposed to touch my space.

Elegant Miami's main art gallery across the MacArthur Causeway was a glittering gem of holiday art.

But over here, at the offices on Miami Beach that had been selected specifically to be near my boss's favorite house, things were toned down. This was where Elegant Miami hid the nitty gritty details of business. It was the safe space for the sales people that spent all day on the phone with overseas clients; it was the home base of the style teams who went and decorated Miami palaces with carefully curated art from around the world; it was a soulless sovereignty of the contracts office where Maureen and I made sure every jot and tittle were in place.

Tittle was one of my coworker's favorite words. It means the dot over a lower case I or J, but it sounds funny. Stuck in an L-shaped, linoleum-floored concrete bunker with two high windows that looked at the neighboring building a foot away and that always smelled of nail polish and mildew, we took our fun where we could find it.

But I drew the line at plastic Naughty Santa window clings blocking the little sunlight available. Being held hostage by forced holiday cheer was not part of my paycheck.

"Happy holidays, Del!" Maureen jumped out from behind my desk wearing a bright blue sweater with silver bells, dancing elves, and snowflakes. The bell at the end of her bright pink Santa hat with pole dancing elves jingled as she stilled.

I stared, carefully counting to ten in every language I could remember, willing the other half the contracts team to vanish. It wasn't enough. Maureen and her seasonal cheer remained where they were.

"Don't you love it? I'm going to spray some fake snow too!" She pointed around at the sad, red tinsel garlands hanging off the black filing cabinets and the tiny palm tree that was sagging under a strand of rainbow lights.

"That's really not necessary," I said carefully circling around the hazardous airspace of the parasitic plant of unwanted kisses.

What was Maureen even thinking? Who on earth was I going to kiss here? It was against my personal policy to kiss clients or married people. That left Rafael Kane, office grinch, as the only possible target of unwanted contact.

Granted, he was a hot and sexy Office Grinch, but he was also the person voted most likely to ruin a party. He didn't chitchat. He didn't get distracted. He didn't waste time talking to coworkers, going to long Friday lunches, or building friendships.

Rafael Kane went to work, smiled for his clients only, and made Elegant Miami over fifteen percent of our yearly profit. We all loved him for his sales acumen and stunning good looks, but no one around here considered him a friend.

Very early on, I'd tried.

But Rafael Kane had taken one look at me, snarled like I'd stabbed his grandma, and avoided me ever since.

Which suited me just fine.

I frowned. If Maureen thought there was any chance of an office romance, my desk would look like an ad for the Great Bridal Expo. I needed tiny white seed pearls and chiffon as much as I needed mistletoe, which was about as much as a shark needed a tuba.

My idea of a good date was streaming a good murder mystery. I liked crime shows, creepy horror movies, and all things Halloween. People joked that I was a pagan, but that wasn't exactly true. I just loved the idea of magic. It made sense to me.

I should have loved the idea of Santa, except I can't remember a time I wasn't poor, and Santa doesn't visit poor kids.

December was my own personal hell. No winter solstice bonfire would ever be big enough to burn away all my anger at the forced cheer, demand for gifts, and unseasonable expectations.

I wasn't making New Year's Resolutions, I did that on my birthday in July.

I wasn't meeting anyone under the mistletoe, I wasn't that desperate.

I wasn't going to participate in the annual gift exchange, because somehow I always wound up with the bar of soap stolen from the pay-by-the-hour motel down the street.

I would be skipping the party, hitting the white sand beaches of Miami with a pink drink in hand, and spending my three days off catching up on N.W. Gehson's *Serial Killerz* series.

Maureen moved out from behind my desk and pouted. All of five-foot-nothing, she was a cute, apple-shaped woman with sunset pink hair and perpetually purple lips from a permanent makeup choice she made thirty years ago when she was twenty-one, drunk, and planning to be an exotic dancer all her life.[37]

In the bright blue sweater, she looked like the world's glummest Sugar Plum Fairy. She was holding a shiny blue paper with the words "All I Want For The Holidays" and a blank space for a holiday wish on it.

If I ignored the paper, I might escape further holiday interrogations.

"I… I was just trying to be nice!" A huge tear shimmered in her eye.

"I know." I patted her shoulder and tried very hard not to look at the tattoo peeking above her collar that HR insisted she keep covered during work hours. "But I don't like Christmas."

"This year is going to be different!" Maureen assured, her smile turning on like a floodlight in turtle season. "I figured out why you don't like Christmas."

"Because it's a commercial farce to celebrate capitalism?"

"No, silly! Because you're single! No one's giving you the good gifts." She winked and tried to bump me with her hip, but since her head only comes up to my shoulder even in kitten heels, it didn't quite work.

I scooted around her and into my three-sided box of an office.

There were sparkly confetti snowflakes covering the nameplate that had been a gift from one of my favorite metalwork artists.

---

[37] She still dances under the name Cotton Candy every other Friday down at the Sugar Strip on 4th, if you're wondering.

Delinna Farmer was not a name that deserved to have snow on it. Especially fake snow.

Shaking the snow off the metal cut-out of my name, I smiled up at Maureen. "Really, Maureen, I'm fine."

"You will be!" She pulled a scroll of candy pink paper out of her cleavage so it unrolled in a long, curling list. "This is Auntie Maureen's list of acceptable bachelors in the greater Miami area."

"Maureen," I said, sitting down and giving her my very best glare, "if Rafael Kane is mentioned even once on that list, I will murder you. Right here and now. There will be blood all over your dancing elf sweater. No jury will convict me."

She rolled her eyes. "Tried that. Obviously there's chemistry there, but Rafe could have chemistry with a doorknob, so it doesn't matter." She put the list of names—written in pink and purple ink—on my desk. "Names. Numbers. Histories. Sizes."

"Siz—Oh!" I covered my mouth. "Sweet mother of pearl! Maureen! This is so invasive!" I crumpled the list up and dropped it in the recycling bin.

"A girl's got to know…"

"I do not need to know anyone's sizes!" I shouted as the door to the contracts office opened and the devil himself walked in.

Rafael's brown eyes went wide, his tan face frozen in a rictus of horror.

"I'm not participating in the company Christmas party and I'm not ordering the shirts," I said loudly, willing Maureen to play along. Rafael might be the office grinch, but nobody gossiped as much as his people in the sales department. If he even guessed at the content of Maureen's list, I'd have every art gallery employee and intern in the greater Miami area sending me extra details.

Maureen, oblivious to the threat of Dick Pic Armageddon, crossed her arms over her ample chest. "Why not? What's wrong with the holiday party?"

"Because..." I scrambled for an excuse that wouldn't insult Maureen's party planning. "...I'm seeing someone."

Rafael snorted in amusement as he shook his head and walked to our copy machine by the door. The sales department had a better one, one that could print posters and banners, but it was broken and the sales associates had been bouncing in and out of the contracts office all week. There was nothing like the holidays to convince the obscenely wealthy to drop hundreds of thousands of dollars on art.

"Oh, sweetie," Maureen said, grabbing my arm and leaning in for a sideways hug as she ignored Rafael. "You don't need to lie."

"I'm not," I lied. "I am in a relationship. And I think it's serious. We're talking about moving in together."

From the copier Rafael gave me a look of disbelief that said, *No one would ever live with you.*

Maureen patted my hand with a tiny sigh of pity. "Let me guess. His name is Nick 'The Closer' Claus and you ordered him from the toys department at Lady Things downtown? I've met him too." Her smile was wicked. "But he doesn't count as a dinner date."

Too. Much. Information.

Closing my eyes, I focused on the filing list I needed to finish today. Anything to get the image of my middle-aged co-worker gleefully bouncing through the adult toy store out of my head.

In my imagination, she wore a frilled pink skirt that barely covered her ample thighs. I shuddered.

My only option was to lie more, or to hope Rafael would step in to help me. "Maureen—"

"No!" Rafael shouted from across the room. "No more. Not until I leave. I do not need to hear this. Let me finish. Please. Five more pages!"

Just for that I wanted to play dirty, but encouraging Maureen would give me a heart attack. There was only one course of action left…

"I'm getting a dog," I said before the dick pics became porno subscriptions in my stocking. "I've been visiting the shelters and I'm planning to adopt one over the holidays."

Maureen's shoulders sagged. "Honey, that does not count."

"A dog will be more loyal than any man will!" I drew myself up, a furious dark queen with a mask of rage perfected after years of studying every campy Halloween vampire movie ever. Morticia Addams, eat your heart out. "Probably more loyal than a woman, too. It'll love me, wait for me, and cuddle with me while I watch horror movies in December. A dog won't make me watch cheesy Christmas specials. A dog will go for walks on the beach with me. A dog will be happy eating whatever I cook—"

"A dog should have a high-protein diet."

Maureen and I both turned to stare.

Had Rafael Kane actually joined a conversation that wasn't about sales? After all these years?

"Do you like dogs?" Maureen asked politely, reverting back to Sweet Office Eccentric like a chameleon. "You've never mentioned them."

Rafael stared at the wall behind the copier as he realized his mistake. His body went rigid and I swear I saw a shiver of terror shimmy through him. He knew Maureen would never let him escape now.

"My mother raised dogs when I was growing up." He finished his copy work and turned to glare at me. "I've seen the stuff you eat for lunch, Del. Do the world a favor and stick to stuffed animals and battery-operated toys. A dog deserves better." He opened his mouth as if he were going to continue, then snapped it shut and marched out, back stiff.

Maureen hummed happily. "He has such a nice tush!"

"Maureen!" I smacked her arm.

"What? I'm married, not dead. I can look."

"We're at work."

"Quitting time was eight minutes ago. I can lust after people off the clock."

"You are a dirty old woman."

"Yes I am," she said proudly.

I rolled my eyes and remembered why I'd come back in. "I need to get my water bottles. I keep forgetting them." Nine of them sat in a row by my spare shoes.

"Oh, is that what happened?" Maureen asked. "I thought you'd decided to decorate with them. Maybe make a shrine to your beloved *agua*."

"Ha ha, funny." I grabbed a big bag with the name of a local farmer's stall on it and stuffed the water bottles inside. "The winter wonderland stuff… Can you keep it off my desk?"

Maureen pouted again.

"Please? I'll bring you some of those spiced pecans you like." If the bodega had a BOGO sale going on. If it wasn't buy-one-get-one, I wasn't sharing.

Her eyes went wide with delight. "Consider it gone. I will leave your corner a natural wasteland of bones, ghouls, and whatever that thing is," she said pointing to my Zany Zombie bobblehead.

"Thank you." I packed up and went home to research animal shelters. If I was going to be forced to participate in the holidays, I deserved to have someone who was happy to see me every day.

Surely I could get a dog for Christmas. It couldn't be that hard.

Keep reading! Head to
www.inkprintpress.com/lianabrooks/
christmas/werewolf/
to buy your copy now!

BODIES IN MOTION
Fleet of Malik Book #1

A civil war tore them apart. Can a cold war bring them back together?

Available from all major retailers.
www.inkprintpress.com/lianabrooks/
malik/bodies/

EVEN VILLAINS FALL IN LOVE
Heroes & Villains Book #1

Can a super villain at the top of his game drop everything to save the woman he loves?

Available from all major retailers.
www.inkprintpress.com/lianabrooks/
heroesandvillains/love/